I0450986

POISON AND PROSE

THE PAGES AND PAWS MYSTERY SERIES

POPPY BRIDGEMAN

Ebook ISBN: 978-1-990509-85-8
Paperback ISBN: 978-1-990509-86-5

Cover created by Getcovers

FREE BOOK

Use the QR code to claim your copy of The Charleston Diary when you sign up for my newsletter. Learn how Ginny solved a case of forgery before she headed to the peace and tranquility of Tidehaven Cove.

1

The late afternoon light streaming through Hampton's Books cast everything in warm honey tones, making even Malcolm's skeptical expression look almost benevolent. Almost. It was Friday, and my test literary tour would officially start tomorrow.

I stood behind the polished oak counter, arranging welcome packets for tomorrow's Devon Literary Walking Tour while trying not to let my excitement show too obviously. Malcolm had already muttered three warnings about American enthusiasm this week.

"The welcome dinner begins at seven," I said, double-checking the sample of the invitation cards Freya made. I'd dropped personalized versions at Mrs. Pengelly's B&B yesterday so our guests would have plenty of time to prepare. The invitation read, Simple meal, wine, chance for everyone to get acquainted before we start walking tomorrow.

"Hmm." Malcolm straightened his bow tie, a gesture I'd learned meant he was weighing whether to voice disapproval. "Your great-aunt would never have considered hosting strangers for dinner among the books."

"My great-aunt also never charged a hundred pounds per person for a literary walking tour," I pointed out, slipping the cards into my pocket. "Times change, Malcolm."

"Indeed they do," he replied, suggesting the changes were deplorable.

Hardy padded over from his favorite spot by the poetry section and pressed his warm corgi bulk against my legs, sensing tension in the air. Austen remained positioned by the front door, her ears pricked forward in surveillance mode. Six months in Tidehaven Cove had taught her that strangers meant either customers with treats or complications that required investigation.

The shop looked particularly welcoming today, if I did say so myself. I'd moved the heavy oak reading table to the center of the main floor and surrounded it with mismatched chairs brought over from my cottage. The display of books by local Devon authors commanded attention from the bay window, and fresh flowers from Dot's garden added splashes of color throughout the space. The familiar scent of old books and furniture polish mixed with the honey-sweet fragrance of late roses, creating an atmosphere that felt both scholarly and inviting.

"Perhaps," Malcolm said, arranging teacups, "we might review the participants' credentials once more? If you are going to ask them to act as specialists in your future tours, you need to be sure."

Well, it couldn't hurt, but it's not like we did deep background checks.

I picked up the registration folder, though I practically had the details memorized. "Dr. Vivienne Sterling, Victorian literature specialist from Oxford. Edmund Fitzmoore, small press publisher. Lily Ashworth, romance novelist researching historical Devon. And Tobias Fletcher, literary researcher. All respectable."

"Mr. Fletcher's research focus remains undefined," Malcolm observed, adjusting his bow tie again. "And Ms. Ashworth's university affiliation appears somewhat vague, most list their college as well as the institution." He lowered his voice. "I mention this because the village communication lines say someone has been asking odd questions. About literary expertise."

For village communication lines, read gossip network.

Before I could ask what he meant, the shop bell chimed. I smoothed my expression into professional warmth, ready to welcome our first literary enthusiast.

Tobias Fletcher stepped through the doorway carrying a battered leather portfolio that he gripped with the intensity of someone protecting state secrets. Middle-aged and rumpled, he looked like someone who'd forgotten to check the mirror before leaving the house. His brown hair stuck up in several directions, and his cardigan had seen better decades, but his eyes missed nothing—scanning the shop with the thoroughness of a professional investigator.

"Mr. Fletcher," I said, stepping forward with what I hoped was the right balance of professional warmth and literary gravitas. "Welcome to Hampton's Books."

"Miss Hampton." His handshake was firm but brief, and his gaze immediately resumed its cataloging of the space. "Fascinating establishment. Heritage buildings often reveal so much about their owners." He withdrew a small digital camera and snapped a photo of the shop interior before producing a leather-bound notebook. "How long has the bookshop been in your family's possession?"

"My great-aunt opened it in 1962," I replied, unnerved by

his clinical approach. This wasn't supposed to be a work session. My experience in managing clients took over and held me back from telling him to relax. "She ran it until her death a little over a year ago."

"1962." He made a careful note, then looked up. "And your book industry background before inheriting? I'm documenting the professional qualifications of everyone involved in Devon's literary tourism industry."

I was already crossing his name off the mental list I'd made of potential experts for the upcoming tours. "I was a senior editor in Charlotte before—"

"Charlotte, North Carolina. American publishing." The dismissal in his voice stung, but I let it go. "Undergraduate degree from...?"

"University of North Carolina." I was beginning to wonder if I was qualifying for a position I didn't want.

"Excellent." He photographed my business license hanging behind the counter. "I trust you won't mind if I verify these credentials? My research requires absolute authentication of all literary professionals' backgrounds."

Something cold settled in my stomach. This felt less like networking and more like being investigated. Before I could ask what research project demanded such thoroughness, Malcolm appeared with his protective instincts clearly activated.

"Perhaps," Malcolm said stiffly, "you might explain the nature of this documentation project?"

Fletcher's smile never wavered. "Academic integrity is crucial in literary circles, wouldn't you agree? I'm compiling a comprehensive database of literary tourism operators. Amazing what public records reveal about authenticity. It will assist tourists who want truth rather than made up stories to entertain them." He focused on Malcolm with predatory interest. "Someone with your experience must understand the importance of verifying credentials. Document authentication, academic affiliations, business registrations—all fascinating research."

Malcolm's posture had gone rigidly formal, a warning sign I'd learned to recognize.

Before Malcolm could respond, the bell chimed again. A woman in her sixties entered with the bearing of someone accustomed to lecture halls and respectful silence. Dr. Vivienne Sterling looked exactly like central casting's version of a distinguished academic—silver hair in a perfect chignon, tailored tweed suit, leather satchel hanging from her left hand.

"Dr. Sterling," I said, grateful for the interruption. "How wonderful to meet you."

"The pleasure is mine." Her accent was crisp BBC English; her handshake confident. "What a charming establishment. I can see why you chose it for our gathering. The atmosphere reminds me of the reading rooms at Balliol. My college at Oxford."

Malcolm tilted his head with polite interest. "How curious—Balliol's not typically associated with Victorian manuscript collections. Wouldn't your research be primarily through the Bodleian?"

Tobias Fletcher immediately pounced, his notebook already open. "Dr. Sterling, perfect timing. I need to document your specific credentials for my database. Your specialization in Victorian manuscript authentication—could you provide your thesis advisor's name and the title of your doctoral dissertation?"

"Indeed," she replied to Malcolm, but something flickered across her face—surprise? Unease? "Though my current research focuses more on narrative themes than technical analysis. Academic bureaucracy, you understand."

"But surely the foundational training remains relevant," Fletcher pressed, photographing her with his digital camera. He acted as if Malcolm didn't exist. "Which authentication protocols do you typically employ? The Morrison technique or the newer Caldwell methodology?"

Dr. Sterling's smile remained composed, but her knuckles whitened where she gripped her handbag. "One employs various... methodologies depending on the material."

Malcolm's eyebrows rose almost imperceptibly. "I imagine someone working with Victorian manuscripts would be quite familiar with the recent Harcourt collection discoveries. Professor Bramwell's authentication work must be invaluable to current research."

Dr. Sterling's pause lasted a heartbeat too long. "Yes, quite... thorough work. I thought this was a social event?"

The conversation felt like verbal fencing, with Fletcher probing systematically while Malcolm's literary expertise inadvertently created pitfalls that caught Dr. Sterling off-guard. I was about to intervene when the bell announced our third arrival.

Edmund Fitzmoore burst through the doorway with slightly frantic energy as if he were perpetually running late, though he was actually five minutes early. He was well-dressed in that shabby-genteel way that suggested financial strain—an expensive suit that had seen too many dry cleanings, shoes that were perfectly polished but resoled multiple times. A briefcase that might have looked leather-bound when new, but now showed cardboard through the worn corners. Everything about him whispered of someone maintaining a professional appearance despite declining circumstances.

"So sorry," he said, slightly out of breath and tugging nervously at his cufflinks. "Traffic in Exeter was murder." He paused, looking embarrassed, then laughed. "Poor choice of words for a mystery tour."

"Not to worry," I assured him. "We're just getting acquainted. Edmund Fitzmoore, meet Tobias Fletcher and Dr. Vivienne Sterling."

"Fitzmoore," Fletcher repeated, this time not making a note. "Fitzmoore & Sons Historical Press—though I believe it's just yourself now, correct? Your publishing house specializes in historical reprints, I believe?"

Edmund's smile became noticeably tighter, and I caught him unconsciously patting his jacket pocket as if checking for something important. "Among other things. We're quite... selective about our projects these days."

"Financial pressures in small press publishing must be considerable," Fletcher observed, photographing Edmund's business card. "I imagine authenticity verification becomes quite expensive when margins are tight."

Edmund's face had gone slightly pale, and he tugged at his cufflinks again—a nervous habit that was becoming more pronounced. "We have our methods," he replied carefully. "Though I find the publishing world can be surprisingly competitive about sharing verification techniques."

Fletcher smirked, only a flash, but it was definitely a knowing expression. "Competitive? In what sense? Are you suggesting corners get cut when financial pressures mount?"

"I didn't say that—"

"Of course not. Though I've been researching the small press industry quite thoroughly. Amazing what financial records reveal about authentication shortcuts." Fletcher leaned forward. "When a press is struggling, the temptation to... shall we call it, expedite processes must be considerable."

Edmund was now actively perspiring despite the cool temperature. "I really don't know what you're implying—"

Before he could finish, our final guest arrived with a jingling of bracelets and a swirl of colorful scarves. Lily Ashworth looked like she'd stepped out of a bohemian fashion magazine—flowing auburn hair, vintage band t-shirt paired with an embroidered jacket, multiple silver rings, and ankle boots that had clearly walked many literary miles.

"I'm so sorry I'm late," she said breathlessly, unwinding herself from various accessories. "I got completely lost in strolling through the village. Everything looks like a postcard."

"You're perfectly on time," I assured her. "Lily Ashworth, our romance novelist. Meet the group."

"Oh wonderful," Lily said, gravitating toward Dr. Sterling. "I'm absolutely dying to hear about your Victorian research. I'm working on a historical romance set in 1870s Devon, and I'm terrified I'll get the details wrong."

"What university did you say you attended?" Fletcher interjected smoothly, his camera already in hand. "Your research methodology must be quite thorough for historical fiction. Could you provide details of your academic credentials for my documentation?"

Lily's cheerful expression faltered slightly. "Oh, you know how it is with writers. We pick up research techniques wherever we can find them. Credentials are for the people on the publishing side. You can't get a PhD in creative thoughts."

"But surely an academic background would provide a

foundation? Even romance writers typically have formal literature training." Fletcher was now photographing her as well, treating her like a specimen to be examined. "Which institution? Graduate or undergraduate degree? I need complete verification of all participants' qualifications."

"Perhaps," Malcolm interjected with perfect timing, "we might move to refreshments? I've prepared the evening meal."

The room had somehow developed an undercurrent of tension that had nothing to do with pre-dinner nerves. I hadn't liked his questions earlier, and now with repetition, they were starting to feel like an interrogation leading to some dark motive.

2

I 'd never been more grateful for Malcolm's formal manners. "Excellent idea. Please, everyone, find a seat."

Fletcher positioned himself where he could observe everyone else, his portfolio never leaving his side. As Malcolm served the meal with ceremonial care. As people took their last bites of the excellent poached salmon with new potatoes and green beans, Fletcher pulled out a manila folder thick with papers.

"I should mention," he said conversationally, spreading some documents on the table and pushing glasses and plates to the side. "I've been researching everyone's backgrounds quite thoroughly. Academic credentials, publication histories, business registrations." He smiled, but it held no warmth, as if someone had shown him how to do it and he'd practiced in the mirror. "It's remarkable how often things don't... align properly."

The room went quiet except for the sound of Malcolm clearing the dishes.

"Research?" Dr. Sterling asked carefully, her wine glass frozen halfway to her mouth.

"Verification research," Fletcher clarified, patting his thick folder. "For my directory. Take small press publishing, for instance." His gaze fixed on Edmund like a laser. "Fascinating how some publishers develop quite creative approaches to fact checking."

Edmund had gone pale and was now gripping his wine glass so tightly I worried it might shatter. "I don't know what you're implying—"

"And university credentials," Fletcher continued, turning to Dr. Sterling. "Sometimes people claim affiliations that prove... difficult to verify through official channels. Oxford, for instance, keeps quite meticulous records of their doctoral graduates but doesn't like to share details."

Dr. Sterling set down her glass with deliberate control. "Mr. Fletcher, what exactly are you suggesting?"

"I'm not suggesting anything. I'm stating facts. Facts I've documented quite thoroughly." He patted his portfolio lovingly. "Evidence, you might say. Amazing what emerges when someone takes the time to properly cross-reference official records."

The word "evidence" hung in the air like a threat.

Edmund stood abruptly, his chair scraping against the wooden floor. "I won't sit here and be accused—"

"Accused of what?" Fletcher asked with false innocence. "I haven't accused anyone. Yet. Though tomorrow's walking tour might prove... enlightening. Particularly our stop at the old church. Amazing what parish records reveal about family histories. And our visit to the manor house—their archives might prove to be a treasure trove."

"You're threatening us," Lily said quietly, her bohemian

cheerfulness completely evaporated. "Don't pretend you aren't. This is ridiculous."

"Threatening? I'm simply conducting thorough research." Fletcher's smile never wavered. "Though I suppose people with nothing to hide wouldn't feel threatened by a few probing questions."

Dr. Sterling rose with dignity, though I could see the tremor in her hands. "This evening has run its course. Thank you for dinner, Miss Hampton. I trust we'll have a more pleasant day tomorrow."

She gathered her things and left, her composure intact but her knuckles white where she gripped her satchel. Edmund followed quickly, muttering about early appointments and urgent calls to make.

Lily lingered, looking genuinely distressed. "I'm so sorry," she said quietly. "This isn't what I expected from a literary tour. I feel like I'm being investigated for some kind of security clearance. I'm a romance writer, not some corporate mole."

After she left, Fletcher remained seated, seemingly satisfied by the evening's collapse. He organized his papers and returned them to his portfolio.

"Well," he said pleasantly, "tomorrow should be interesting. I do hope everyone's prepared for some... revelations. My research is quite comprehensive, you know. People will be amazed what I've uncovered about their backgrounds."

I didn't want a repeat of tonight's performance. "Mr. Fletcher, this is a tour of literary locations in the area. I do hope you are planning to enjoy the event in the way it was planned. This is a test of the concept. I was rather hoping to find a few experts who would be willing to help future sessions. Ones targeted toward tourists interested in a little history. Not people looking for a witch hunt."

"A little mystery and suspense will add some spice to the tour, don't you think?" He left before I could say no to his idea of seasoning the carefully planned walks and teas.

When he was gone, Malcolm and I stood in the sudden silence, surrounded by abandoned wine glasses and the wreckage of what should have been a pleasant literary evening.

"Well," Malcolm said, straightening his bow tie with deliberate precision, "that was illuminating."

"That was a disaster."

"Perhaps. Though I suspect Mr. Fletcher's research extends well beyond academic curiosity." Malcolm began collecting the abandoned place settings. "That was intimidation disguised as fact finding."

The door opened again, making us both jump. I turned, expecting Fletcher to return with another cryptic threat, but instead found myself face-to-face with the last person I'd expected to see in Tidehaven Cove.

"Surprise!" Beau Morrison stood in the doorway, perfectly pressed despite what must have been hours of travel, holding a bouquet of roses and wearing the charming smile that had once made my heart race. "Hope you're ready for company!"

I stared at him, feeling the last of the evening's equilibrium desert me. My charming workaholic ex-boyfriend, who'd spent three years choosing his career over our relationship. The man I'd finally gotten over. Mostly.

"Beau." I couldn't manage more than his name.

"I know, I know, I should have called. But I wanted to surprise you. I've been thinking about us, Ginny, and I realized I made a terrible mistake letting you go." His gaze swept the shop, taking in the intimate dinner setup, the wine glasses, Malcolm's formal attire. "Did I interrupt something important?"

Malcolm cleared his throat diplomatically. "I believe I'll tidy up in the back," he murmured, disappearing with admirable speed.

I looked down at Hardy and Austen, who had positioned themselves on either side of my feet like furry bodyguards, sensing trouble in their uncanny way.

"What do you think?" I asked them. "Ready for another adventure?"

3

———

My phone rang at seven in the morning, jarring me from uneasy dreams about leather portfolios and probing questions.

"Ginny," Mrs. Pengelly's voice was tight with worry. "I'm dreadfully sorry to ring so early, but I caught Mr. Fletcher coming out of Dr. Sterling's room with her papers. He had a torch and was photographing documents with his mobile phone."

I sat up in bed instantly alert. "He was photographing her papers?"

"It looked like her CV, university transcripts, everything from her manuscript folder. When I challenged him, he claimed Dr. Sterling had asked him to review her academic references for accuracy." Mrs. Pengelly's voice shook. "But she was still asleep, Ginny. I'd just delivered morning tea to all the rooms."

Austen and Hardy were already on their feet, reading the tension in my voice. "Did you confront him directly?"

"I told him guests weren't allowed in each other's rooms, and he became quite cold. Started asking whether I'd explained the rules before accepting their bookings. Mentioned something about frauds playing at experts."

Still on his bandwagon. "That sounds like justifying nosiness."

"When I dropped off his tea, I had to move some things for the cup and plate of biscuits. He had a notebook full of information about your tour participants—things he shouldn't know. Specific details about their educational backgrounds, employment histories. Ginny, this isn't normal behavior for a guest in my establishment."

"We'll be there straightaway," I said, already pulling on clothes. "Keep an eye on him, but don't get too close."

I was fastening my coat when someone knocked at my door. The confident rap was followed by a familiar voice calling out cheerfully.

"Ginny? I know it's early, but I heard you talking and thought I might join you for breakfast, or take you to the cafe."

I'd insisted he stay with me, in the guest room of course, but I'd forgotten he was here when I got the call.

"Beau." I grabbed my keys, my mind still processing Mrs. Pengelly's information. "I'd normally love to have a full English breakfast with you, but I have a situation developing."

I saw from the change in expression from friendly to focused that his crisis management instincts engaged at once. "What kind of situation?"

"One of my literary tour participants has been investigating the others. Photographing their credentials, researching their backgrounds." I started down the stairs. "Come on, you might actually be useful for this."

"Wouldn't be the first mysterious situation I've helped you sort out," he said, following me toward the village green.

Hardy and Austen bounded ahead, their alert attention suggesting they sensed the morning's urgency. As we crossed toward Harbor Road, another figure approached from the direction of the waterfront.

Elliot emerged from the early morning mist carrying a manila folder, his expression shifting from professional purpose to surprise as he noticed my companion. His Land Rover sat parked near the bookshop entrance.

"Ginny." His gray-blue eyes moved between Beau and me, taking in the closeness and making assumptions. "I brought those coastal safety maps for today's walk. Everything all right?"

"Dr. Harrington, you remember Beauregard Morrison from Charleston," I said briskly.

The two men shook hands and followed me. "What's the emergency?" Elliot asked.

"Tobias Fletcher has been caught searching other guests' rooms and photographing their academic credentials. Mrs. Pengelly found him with Dr. Sterling's transcripts and CV."

Both men's expressions sharpened with concern.

"That's not random behavior," Beau said. "Someone conducting that level of background research has a specific purpose. And I'd say it has nothing to do with the tour you've arranged."

"Agreed," Elliot said. "Should we call the police? He may have broken in to obtain his information."

"Not yet. Let's assess the situation first." I quickened my pace toward the B&B. "But this explains yesterday's interrogations about everyone's university backgrounds and thesis advisers."

Mrs. Pengelly met us at her kitchen door, still in her dressing gown and clearly shaken. "He's in the dining room with the other guests, acting as though nothing happened. But he's been asking a lot of questions since I called you."

"What questions specifically?" I asked.

"When I say asking, that's all he did. He tried to engage the others in conversation, and they avoided him. It certainly looked like they didn't want him around. And he didn't get any answers. I think your walk today will be a bit tense."

Through the dining room window, I could see Tobias Fletcher calmly buttering toast while Dr. Sterling sat across from him.

"Did you tell her what he did?" I asked. "You say she was asleep when he was coming out of her room?"

"I didn't think it was my place," Mrs. Pengelly said. "It isn't as bad as you make it sound. She has a suite. I'm sure he just slipped into the sitting area, not her bedroom."

"Has he shown interest in other guests' belongings?" Beau asked.

"Yesterday I noticed him lingering near the key rack when guests went out for dinner."

Austen pressed against my leg, her body rigid with attention focused on Tobias through the window. Hardy positioned himself beside her, both dogs radiating the alert stillness they'd learned during previous village mysteries.

"The dogs don't like him," I observed.

"They are smart dogs," Mrs. Pengelly said firmly.

A raised voice from inside made us all turn toward the window. Tobias was standing now, leaning forward over the table toward Dr. Sterling with obvious aggression.

"We need to intervene," I said.

We slipped through the back door and positioned ourselves where we could hear the breakfast room conversation clearly.

"—your Oxford dissertation adviser, Professor Hennessey, seems to have no record of supervising any doctoral students in Victorian literature during the 1980s," Tobias was saying, his tone clinical and accusatory.

"That is none of your business." Dr. Sterling's face had gone pale. "I don't know where you're getting your information, but—"

"From Oxford's official records, which are quite comprehensive. Your supposed thesis committee also presents some interesting inconsistencies when cross-referenced with university employment records."

"This is outrageous!" Dr. Sterling's voice shook with what sounded like fear rather than anger. "You have no right to investigate my academic background!"

Edmund Fitzmoore shifted uncomfortably in his chair. "Perhaps we could discuss literary topics instead of personal credentials?"

Tobias turned toward him with a slight smile. "Interesting that you'd prefer avoiding discussions of credentials, Mr. Fitzmoore. Particularly given the... creative approach to fact checking that small press publishers sometimes employ."

Edmund's coffee cup rattled against its saucer. "I don't know what you're implying."

"Nothing specific. Simply observing that independent presses might be less rigorous about verifying authors' claimed qualifications than, say, university publishers."

I noticed Lily Ashworth had set down her newspaper and was watching the exchange, focused so tightly it was like she was trying to impress her mind with mental notes. Her expression held none of the confusion or alarm I'd expect from a romance novelist witnessing an academic dispute. Was she thinking of using this in one of her books? Perhaps a disagreement between rival dukes?

"Gentlemen, please," Dr. Sterling said, her voice barely steady. "This is neither the time nor place for such discussions."

"On the contrary," Tobias replied, "transparency about academic credentials should be welcome anywhere serious literature is discussed. Unless, of course, one has reason to prefer obscurity on such matters."

The silence that followed was thick with tension. Dr. Sterling's hands were visibly trembling, while Edmund stared into his coffee as though seeking escape.

I stepped into the dining room with a bright, professional smile. "Good morning, everyone! I hope Mrs. Pengelly's taking excellent care of you. I wanted to confirm our departure time for the coastal walk—nine-thirty sharp from the harbor."

The relief on Dr. Sterling's face was immediate and profound. Edmund managed a weak smile, while Lily nodded with what seemed like genuine gratitude for the interruption.

Only Tobias looked annoyed by my arrival.

"Miss Hampton," he said with forced courtesy. "Perfect timing. Perhaps you could share your vetting procedures for tour participants?"

"Vetting procedures?" I kept my tone light while noting the fear in Dr. Sterling's eyes. "We're a walking tour focused on enjoying literature and beautiful scenery, Mr. Fletcher. Not an academic conference requiring peer review. The only research I did was in service of making sure my participants enjoyed the experience. "

"But surely responsible tour operators verify that their

guest experts possess the credentials they claim? Dr. Sterling's supposed Oxford doctorate, for instance?"

Dr. Sterling's cup rattled against its saucer, and I noticed Edmund had gone extremely pale.

"I trust my participants to represent themselves honestly," I said firmly. "Just as I assume that writers joining literary tours are interested in books rather than conducting unauthorized background investigations of fellow guests."

Tobias's eyes narrowed. "You're suggesting I'm not a legitimate author?"

"I'm suggesting that questioning people's academic credentials over breakfast isn't typical behavior for someone here to enjoy poetry, novels, and coastal walks."

Behind me, I sensed Beau and Elliot positioning themselves near the doorway—not territorially, but with the practical coordination of two professionals supporting a colleague in a difficult situation.

"Perhaps," Lily Ashworth said smoothly, "we could focus on the literary aspects of our tour? I'm particularly interested in how local folklore influenced the Romantic poets."

It was expertly done—redirecting attention while giving everyone a graceful exit from the confrontation.

Dr. Sterling nodded gratefully. "Yes, that would be much more appropriate."

Edmund managed to straighten in his chair. The move changed his manner from frightened to calm as if he'd chosen to take his side with the two women. "Absolutely. Local literary history is why we're here."

Only Tobias looked unsatisfied, but seemed to realize he'd lost the bid for control. "Of course. Though I maintain that authenticity should be valued in all contexts—literary, academic, or otherwise."

"Transparency is indeed important," I agreed. "Speaking

of which, I'd love to hear more about your own work, Mr. Fletcher. Your new foray into procedurals—what specific themes are you exploring?"

For the first time, Tobias Fletcher looked genuinely uncomfortable. "It's... still in the research phase. Quite complex subject matter."

"I'm sure it is," I said pleasantly. "Well, shall we meet at the harbor in an hour? The tide will be perfect for exploring the smugglers' walks."

As the group began to disperse, Dr. Sterling approached me with obvious desperation. "Miss Hampton, could I speak with you privately? It's quite urgent."

Perhaps she was about to share something that would defuse the situation once and for all. "Of course."

She glanced around to ensure we weren't overheard. "That man—his questions are far too specific. He knows details about my background that aren't publicly available. Academic records that would require official access to verify."

That was not news; we'd all heard the accusations last night. "What kind of details?"

"My dissertation committee members, the exact dates of my thesis defense, even discrepancies in university employment records." Her voice dropped to a whisper. "Miss Hampton, I think he's some kind of professional investigator. And I think he's found evidence that my academic credentials aren't... entirely authentic."

This was the same as Mrs. Pengelly reported, so I was inclined to believe her. If she was worried, perhaps there was some truth to Fletcher's efforts. "Are they authentic?"

Dr. Sterling's expression was answer enough. "It's complicated. I can explain, but not here. Could we talk privately later?"

"Of course. But are you in danger?"

"I don't know. But Miss Hampton, I'm not the only one. Look at how Edmund reacted when Tobias mentioned small press fact checking. And did you notice how carefully Lily was watching everyone? She was taking mental notes like a journalist, not listening like a romance novelist."

As she hurried away, I found myself facing Beau and Elliot, who'd been waiting with patient concern.

"Professional investigator conducting background checks on academic credentials," Beau said quietly. "Dr. Sterling has a point. I can't think why a journalist would be interested in a hard hitting article about your experts. But he's not acting like an author, either. You do attract some odd types, Ginny."

"It's not Ginny's fault," Elliot said. "Either way, he's not what he claimed to be. The question is whether he's exposing fraud or planning to exploit it."

"Our next step," I said, surprised to realize I meant the plural, "is to keep him under close observation during today's coastal walk. And find out exactly what kind of secrets my literary tour participants are hiding."

As we left Mrs. Pengelly's B&B, both dogs fell into step beside us with the alert attention of partners in investigation. I couldn't help thinking that my peaceful literary walking tour to test out a few experts had just become a very different kind of mystery.

4

Yesterday, the exploration of the paths smugglers took to disperse their booty had gone well. The discussion of life in Victorian times for writers was refreshing and invigorating. Mr. Fletcher kept his intrusive questions and insinuations to himself. Or rather, I did a good job of redirecting the conversation every time he tried to bring his 'directory' up.

The village network in Tidehaven Cove rivaled any intelligence service, and by this morning, it was buzzing with reports of someone conducting unauthorized inquiries about our literary tour participants.

I discovered this when I stopped by Elspeth's tea shop at seven-thirty, hoping for a peaceful tea before the day began. Instead, I found myself recruited into what could only be described as an emergency consultation.

"Ginny, dear!" Elspeth called from behind the counter, where she was arranging a display of literary-themed tea blends. "Perfect timing. We've been comparing notes about your Mr. Fletcher, and the picture isn't encouraging."

Shirley sat at a corner table with Dot Jenkins and Mrs.

Chen from the village post office, all three speaking in the hushed tones reserved for serious village business. Mrs. Chen's usually cheerful demeanor had been replaced by obvious concern, while Shirley looked like someone who'd spent the night dealing with increasingly problematic guest behavior.

"Sit down," Shirley said firmly, gesturing toward an empty chair that had obviously been saved for me. "You need to hear what we've discovered."

"Oh, my dear," Shirley began, shaking her head with worry and a little of delight at having hot gossip. "That man has been prowling about at all hours. I caught him on the phone at midnight—couldn't help but hear him from the hall, speaking quite urgently to someone. Then this morning I found him in the front parlor with his torch, taking photographs."

This was new. "Photographs?"

"My guest registry. Bold as brass, photographing the signatures and addresses of everyone who's stayed with me this past year." Shirley's tone suggested this ranked somewhere between bad manners and actual criminality. "When I asked what he was doing, he claimed he was researching local literary connections. As if the guest book at a B&B would contain literary anything! I made him delete the photos. He was not happy with that."

Dot leaned forward, lowering her voice conspiratorially. "I saw him yesterday evening, walking, well, I'd call it skulking if I was being truly honest. Not a proper country-side stroll, mind you—more like someone taking note of who was coming and going."

Elspeth appeared with Earl Grey and fresh scones, settling herself at our table with a satisfied air, getting ready to share important intelligence. "He was in here yesterday, asking pointed questions. As if we'd know the answers about what they get up to in Oxford."

"That could be normal interest," I said, hoping to take the speculation off the boil. Of course it didn't really make any sense, and no one bought it.

"Perhaps," Shirley replied doubtfully. "But when I mentioned Mr. Fletcher's questions to Dr. Sterling, she went quite pale. Claimed a sudden headache and spent the rest of the evening in her room."

"Then there's Mr. Fitzmoore," Dot added, consulting a small notebook she'd produced from her cardigan. "Yesterday morning he was asking Tom if there was a package for him to pick up. Seemed nervous about it—kept looking around as if he didn't want to be overheard asking."

I accepted tea and a warm scone, grateful for the comfort food while processing this information. I took a little of the cream and spread it before adding a dollop of jam. I'd been admonished for doing it the opposite way the first day I ate here.

Through the window, I could see Hampton's Books across the green, its familiar blue door catching the morning sunlight. Malcolm would be arriving soon, and I should be there to help prepare for whatever the day might bring.

"He said it was for his publishing business, but Tom thought he seemed rather anxious about the whole thing."

Elspeth nodded sagely. "And Mr. Fletcher has been in here twice, asking about parish records and local historical documents. Very specific questions about how to verify family histories and educational backgrounds."

I was definitely regretting my decision to invite him. "What did you tell him?"

"That he'd need to speak to the church secretary and the

county records office. But honestly, Ginny, his questions felt more like a job interview than simple interest." Elspeth paused to butter a scone—apparently being a Devon native for generations, allowed her to do what she wished. "Is your tour an excuse for a new investigation, Ginny? Something fishy in the literary world?"

"It is simply the first test of something Oliver and I thought would be fun." My business neighbor and local antiques specialist, had bullied me into the idea. The first session was run for experts to test out the content. "We're going to publish the schedule on the tourist site. Nothing more than a business proposition."

Although, Oliver had used his recovery from a broken leg as an excuse to let me do all the work. I had enjoyed all the planning even though I grumbled a bit at his absence. He'd even left the day before our participants arrived for a three-day spa vacation.

I thought about yesterday and the start of this odd side track from Mr. Fletcher. "Has anyone actually seen what's in that portfolio he guards so carefully?" I asked.

"Not the contents," Dot replied, "but I can tell you he treats it like precious cargo. Yesterday I offered to hold it while he tied his shoelace, and he practically clutched it to his chest."

"He keeps mentioning having discovered interesting inconsistencies in people's professional backgrounds," Shirley added with obvious distaste. "Claims he's found evidence of... well, he wasn't specific, but the implications weren't pleasant. It's important to him, but he doesn't understand we couldn't be less interested."

Soon tour participants would gather for our pre-walk literary discussion. The contrast between the peaceful village scene and our growing concerns about Tobias felt surreal. Since he'd let it go yesterday, I could only hope that would continue today.

"Ladies," I said, standing and reaching for my purse, "I appreciate all this information, but please be careful around Mr. Fletcher. If he's really investigating people's backgrounds, he might not react well to knowing you're watching him."

"Oh, don't worry about us," Dot said cheerfully, patting my hand with maternal reassurance. "We've been keeping an eye on odd characters since before that man was born. Village life, you know."

"Besides," Elspeth added, beginning to clear the tea things, "if he causes any real trouble, the whole community will know about it. Nobody bothers residents of Tidehaven Cove without dealing with all of us."

5

Back at Hampton's Books, I found Malcolm arranging chairs in the main reading area for our morning literary discussion. Austen and Hardy trotted over to greet him, tails wagging, before settling into their favorite spot near the fireplace where they could monitor all shop activity.

"Good morning," Malcolm said, glancing up from his chair arrangements. "I trust the village intelligence network has been active this morning?"

"How did you know where I'd been?" I asked, though I was no longer surprised by his uncanny awareness of village happenings.

"Mrs. Willoughby's Earl Grey has a distinctive aroma," he replied with the faintest hint of a smile. "And given yesterday's... developments... it seemed likely you'd seek community consultation."

I settled behind the counter, appreciating the familiar comfort of the bookshop's atmosphere—the scent of old paper and furniture polish, the morning light streaming through windows, the dogs' contented sighs from their hearth spot. "What's your assessment of Mr. Fletcher?"

Malcolm straightened, adjusting a poetry collection on the nearby display table. "He visited yesterday evening, after you'd left for the day. Claimed interest in our local history section, but his questions were rather more personal than scholarly."

"Personal how?"

"He wanted to know about our tour participants— whether they'd visited the shop before, how well we knew them." Malcolm's expression showed polite disapproval. "I informed him that customer privacy is quite sacred at Hampton's Books."

Trust Malcolm to come up with a plausible reason to avoid gossip outside the grapevine. "How did he take that?"

"About as well as one might expect He does seem like a man accustomed to getting his way through persistence rather than charm." Malcolm began organizing the morning's book display. "He suggested that literary communities should be more... transparent about qualifications."

The shop bell chimed, and we both looked toward the entrance. Not Tobias, who I expected to appear when we spoke of him, much like the devil. Beau stepped through the doorway, looking refreshed and cheerful.

"Morning, Ginny. You look lovely as usual," he said, his Charleston accent warming the greeting. "Thought I'd stop by before your coastal adventure and see if there's anything I can do to help."

The sight of him should have been reassuring, but instead I felt that familiar mixture of affection and exasperation that had characterized our relationship for three years. Beau had an excellent talent for appearing when things were manageable and disappearing when they became complicated. With the exception of work. For a business call he'd drop everything else.

"Actually, yes," I said, grateful for the offer. "Could you help me carry some books for the coastal walk? We're bringing poetry collections that relate to Devon landscapes."

"My pleasure." Beau moved toward the display table, then paused as Hardy trotted over to investigate the newcomer. "Well, hello there, handsome fellow."

Hardy, never one to resist compliments, immediately offered his paw for shaking. Beau crouched down to greet both dogs, which earned him several points in my mental ledger. Austen, more reserved in her judgments, allowed a brief ear scratch before returning to her fireplace vigil.

"They're excellent judges of character," Malcolm observed with approval. "Hardy's never wrong about people."

"Good to know I pass the test," Beau said, straightening up. "What time does your literary expedition begin?"

"Ten-thirty at the harbor. We're walking to the smugglers' caves for atmospheric readings and historical context." I began selecting books from our Devon poetry collection. "Should be a lovely morning for it."

"Mind if I tag along? I've been meaning to explore more of the coastline, and it sounds more appealing than reading quarterly reports in your kitchen."

The request pleased me more than it should have. Despite our complicated history, Beau's presence always made challenging situations feel more manageable. "Of course. Fair warning—you might be recruited to carry more than just my books. You may need to apply a few of your diplomatic skills if things get difficult."

He took the challenge seriously. "Difficult how? Do you have a saboteur?"

Before I could explain about Tobias's increasingly strange behavior, the shop bell chimed again. This time it admitted Dr. Sterling, looking elegant but slightly tense in her walking clothes and sturdy boots. "Good morning," she said as though she hadn't been involved in Tobias' interrogations. "I hope I'm not too early for our discussion."

"Perfect timing," I assured her, gesturing toward the arranged chairs. "Coffee? Or, perhaps, tea?"

"I'm from the city, so coffee is my sin. Strong, if you have it."

One of the first changes I made was to install an espresso machine. I'd ordered it after I saw that Malcolm's version of strong coffee was an extra spoonful of instant.

As I prepared her drink, I noticed Dr. Sterling glancing around the shop appreciating our collections. She paused at our classic literature section, running her fingers along the spines with obvious pleasure.

"What a wonderful collection," she said. "Your great-aunt clearly had excellent taste. These early editions of Dickens are particularly nice."

"Feel free to browse," I said, handing her a steaming mug. "That's what they're here for."

Malcolm added fresh pastries from the village bakery to the assortment already on the table, and for a few minutes, the shop filled with the comfortable atmosphere of people who loved books gathering to share that appreciation. Dr. Sterling seemed to relax, discussing Victorian publishing practices with Malcolm while Beau examined our local interest section.

It did make me wonder how we would host a similar event with tourists and experts. To make this profitable, we'd either need to charge much more, or to limit the number of people. That was something I'd make Oliver work out. He couldn't just be the ideas man.

For now, I would just enjoy a peaceful literary morning. The sort of thing I'd envisioned when planning the tour.

Unfortunately, it didn't last.

The bell chimed again, admitting Edmund Fitzmoore with an apologetic smile and slightly out-of-breath appearance.

"Sorry I'm running late," he said, checking his watch. "Phone call from London that went longer than expected."

"Business troubles?" Beau asked with professional sympathy. "I know how publishing works. It's not all reading and approving marketing plans. Just like any big enterprise, it's a lot of normal business crises and glad handing."

"Yes. The usual challenges of independent publishing. We may not be multinational, but the same things apply," Edmund replied diplomatically, though I noticed the worried crease between his eyebrows. "Cash flow, manuscript deadlines, the eternal struggle of small presses. Just fewer people to carry the load."

Malcolm offered him coffee, and soon we had a comfortable group discussing the morning's literary themes. In his role as local curator of the historic books, he'd prepared an excellent overview of Devon poets and their connection to coastal landscapes. To my surprise, Beau proved surprisingly knowledgeable about regional history.

"I had no idea Charleston had such strong connections to Devon literary traditions," Dr. Sterling remarked. "The maritime trade routes must have facilitated quite a bit of cultural exchange."

"More than most people realize," Beau agreed. "Ginny's

expertise in historical publishing helped me appreciate those connections."

The compliment warmed me more than it should have, especially given our complicated history. Across the shop, I caught Malcolm's approving nod at Beau's respectful references to my professional background.

Twenty minutes before our scheduled departure, Lily Ashworth arrived looking slightly flustered but as colorfully dressed as ever. She'd clearly prepared for coastal walking with practical boots and a weather-resistant jacket, though she'd maintained her signature style with flowing scarves and jingling bracelets.

"Sorry, sorry!" she called, unwinding herself from various accessories. "I got completely lost trying to find the footpath that leads to the harbor. This village is like a maze if you're not used to it."

"No worries," I assured her. "We're just finishing our discussion of coastal poetry. Would you like coffee before we head out?"

"Tea, if you have it. Coffee tends to dehydrate me. Isn't that odd for something that's mostly water."

"I agree?" Edmund said with a smile. "Even a gently hike can affect you if you aren't properly prepared."

"I know, but that's a story for our social time. Those cliffs look rather dramatic from here. I'm more of a city person—give me busy streets over rural precipices any day."

Dr. Sterling laughed. "The paths are perfectly safe if you stay on the marked routes. I've done quite a bit of coastal walking."

As the group chatted about hiking experiences and literary inspiration, I felt the earlier tension beginning to ease. Perhaps my concerns about Tobias had been overblown. Maybe today would simply be a pleasant literary expedition after all. He'd seemed able to put aside his questions during the previous outings.

The next entrance wasn't Fletcher as expected, but Elliot. He arrived carrying his veterinary bag and looking professionally competent in walking gear. His appearance shouldn't have flustered me, but the sight of him always made me acutely aware of the unresolved feelings I'd been trying to ignore.

"Dr. Harrington," I said, hoping my voice sounded more composed than I felt. "Thank you for joining us."

"Wouldn't miss it," he replied with his characteristic understated smile. "Coastal walks can be unpredictable, and it seemed prudent to have medical expertise available. I am capable of providing basic first aid to humans." He patted his bag. "Filled this with what we might need."

"Beau's joining our expedition," I explained, aware that I was probably overcompensating with cheerful enthusiasm. "He's interested in Devon's literary connections."

"Excellent," Elliot said mildly. "The more perspectives, the better."

Hardy trotted over to greet Elliot, tail wagging with the enthusiastic recognition reserved for favored humans. Austen followed more sedately, allowing a dignified ear scratch before returning to her position as shop supervisor.

As we prepared to leave for the harbor, gathering books and supplies for the coastal walk, I couldn't shake the feeling that the day's dynamics had shifted in ways I didn't entirely understand. Tobias Fletcher who hadn't yet joined us, so I was unsure of how he would be acting.

Still, standing in the morning sunlight with a group of book lovers preparing to explore Devon's beautiful coastline, I felt cautiously optimistic. Perhaps some fresh air and dramatic scenery would put everything in perspective.

6

At ten-thirty, our group gathered at the harbor steps for the coastal walk. The morning had turned out perfectly—sunny but not too warm, with a gentle breeze that carried the scent of sea salt and wild flowers. The dramatic Devon coastline stretched invitingly in both directions, offering exactly the sort of atmospheric setting that made walking tours memorable.

"Right then," I said, addressing our assembled group. "We'll be following the coastal path toward Hangman's Cove, where we'll explore more cave systems that inspired local smuggling legends. The walk takes about ninety minutes, with stops for poetry readings and historical context."

Tobias Fletcher joined us at the very last minute, his ever-present portfolio now secured in a weather-resistant bag and carried over his shoulder to leave his hands free. He looked around the group with what I was beginning to recognize as calculating assessment rather than literary enthusiasm.

"Perfect weather for exploration," he said pleasantly.

"I'm particularly looking forward to the caves. Such atmospheric locations tend to inspire... illuminating discussions."

Something about his tone made the comment sound less innocent than it should have, but before I could respond, Elliot was explaining the safety protocols for coastal walking.

"The paths are well-maintained, but please watch your footing near cliff edges," he said with authority. "We'll stay together as a group, and if anyone feels uncertain about the terrain, just speak up."

"Sage advice," Beau agreed. "Beautiful as it is, this coastline demands respect."

As we set off along the cliff path, I found myself walking between Beau and Elliot—a positioning that felt both natural and slightly awkward. Beau kept up easy conversation about the landscape and local history, while Elliot provided practical observations about coastal wildlife and safety considerations.

Behind us, Dr. Sterling and Edmund walked together, discussing Victorian travel literature with genuine enthusiasm. Lily brought up the rear with Tobias, though I noticed her animated chatter seemed forced, as if she were working hard to maintain a cheerful conversation. Tobias didn't seem to be feeling talkative.

The first part of the walk was genuinely lovely. The coastal path wound along dramatic cliff tops offering spectacular views, while the group maintained light chatter I'd hoped for when planning the tour. Malcolm had provided excellent background material about Devon poets and their coastal inspiration, and even Tobias contributed some interesting observations about maritime literature. Perhaps he'd taken the hint about his behavior.

With the stops to point out views and points of interest,

we were twenty minutes into what would normally be a five-minute journey when we paused at a particularly scenic viewpoint where local legends claimed smugglers had once signaled to ships at sea. I was reading from a collection of Devon poetry when Elliot's phone buzzed.

"I'm sorry," he said, checking the message. "Veterinary emergency back in the village. I should return immediately."

"Of course," I said, though his departure left me feeling unexpectedly vulnerable. "We'll be careful on the cliffs."

As Elliot took a first aid kit out of his bag and handed it to Beau with instructions on how to use it. Then he headed back toward the village.

Our group continued along the coastal path toward Hangman's Cove. The mood had shifted subtly. As if we'd been in a different reality and now our day-to-day worries had intruded and broken some kind of spell.

"Well," Tobias said cheerfully as we approached the cave entrance, "that was educational. Amazing how many dangers lurk in an innocent English village. Perhaps I should venture into mysteries rather than thrillers. My genre tends toward exotic modes of killing. I understand almost everything in a garden is poisonous at the right dosage."

Where had that come from? Ah, one of the poems mentioned lily-of-the-valley as stealing love. His tone suggested he found the whole topic rather amusing, which did nothing to restore my confidence about the wisdom of trusting him to behave.

The caves themselves were spectacular—natural chambers carved by centuries of tidal action, with openings that framed dramatic views of the churning sea beyond. Perfect for poetry readings and historical discussion about smuggling legends. At low tide, of course.

As our group explored the main chamber, I found myself watching Tobias more carefully. His questions about the caves seemed normal enough—inquiring about historical uses, commenting on the acoustic properties, taking photographs of the dramatic rock formations. But there was something calculating in his attention to the group, as if he were assessing opportunities rather than appreciating scenery.

"Tomorrow morning's planned activities should be interesting as well," he said conversationally as we prepared to head back. "Mrs. Pengelly serves an excellent breakfast to her guests. Perfect opportunity for... stimulating conversation."

I'd arranged for our discussion to be over a meal at the B&B tomorrow. We were almost at the end of the agenda for the tour. I thought the opportunity was perfect for some feedback.

Dr. Sterling and Edmund exchanged another of those loaded glances, while Lily suddenly became very interested in examining seashells near the cave entrance.

"The literary discussion continues tomorrow," I said firmly. "That's what we're here for."

"Of course," Tobias agreed with that same pleasant smile that somehow managed to feel threatening. "Though I suspect tomorrow's discussions might prove more... revelatory than today's."

As we made our way back along the coastal path in the golden afternoon light, I couldn't shake the feeling that whatever Tobias Fletcher was planning, it was building toward something that would happen soon. The peaceful literary tour atmosphere felt increasingly fragile, like a stage set waiting for the real drama to begin.

Still, the day had passed without serious incident, the caves had been genuinely impressive, and perhaps my concerns were overblown. Tomorrow we'd return to the safety of the village, where community eyes could keep watch and Malcolm's steady presence could help maintain civilized behavior.

7

T he phone rang before the sun fully rose, dragging me from restless dreams filled with leather portfolios and midnight whispers. Shirley Pengelly's voice came through the line, shaky and wrong—nothing like her usual brisk efficiency.

"Ginny? Oh dear, I'm so sorry to ring so early, but I... I don't know what to do. It's Mr. Fletcher. Something's happened."

I sat up, instantly awake. Austen and Hardy lifted their heads from their beds, sensing trouble. "What kind of something?"

"I think he's... oh, Ginny, I think he might be dead."

The words hit me like cold water. As annoying and slightly frightening as he was, Tobias didn't deserve to die. I know some fatal conditions are hidden, but he'd seemed healthy. "Are you sure?"

"I brought his morning tea at half past six—he always insisted on that exact time, very particular about his routine. When he didn't answer my knock, I thought perhaps he'd overslept, but I could see his light was on from the glow under the door." Her voice cracked. "I used my master key and found him just sitting there at the little desk. He's not... he won't wake up."

Heart attack? Stroke? "Have you called for help?"

"I rang 999 first thing. They said not to touch anything and someone would be right along. But I don't know what to tell the other guests when they wake up, and what about breakfast, and—"

I couldn't leave her to deal with this by herself. And those other guests were just as much my responsibility as hers. "Shirley, take a breath. I'm coming over right now."

I scrambled into the first clothes I found. Black pants and a cream sweater, my hands shaking as I brushed my hair. While I hoped for natural causes, part of me worried Tobias had been killed. I prayed that it wasn't happening. Not again. Not in our peaceful village. I left a note for Beau and then headed to the B&B.

The early morning air was soft and misty as I crossed the green with both dogs. Tidehaven Cove looked exactly as it had every other morning—fishing boats bobbing in the harbor, seagulls wheeling overhead, the first wisps of smoke rising from cottage chimneys. Normal. Peaceful. Nothing like a place where people died unexpectedly.

Shirley was waiting by her kitchen door, wearing a coat over her night dress. Her silver hair, usually so perfectly arranged, stuck up at odd angles.

"Oh, thank goodness you're here," she said, clutching my arm. "I didn't know who else to call. It's all so dreadful."

She led me inside, talking in rapid bursts. "He wanted his tea early, you see. Always six-thirty sharp. Said writers needed to catch the morning thoughts before they escaped. Seemed a bit odd, but guests have their ways, don't they? Writers aren't bound by regular hours."

We climbed the narrow stairs, Shirley's hand gripping the banister. "I knocked and knocked, but there was no answer. His light had been on since I got up at five—I could see it from my kitchen window. That's what worried me. Who works that late and then that early?"

Outside Tobias's door, she stopped, suddenly reluctant. "I shouldn't have opened it, should I? But what if he'd fallen, or had a heart attack and needed help? You read about people lying there for days..."

Through the crack in the door, I could see a figure hunched over the small writing desk by the window. Even from this angle, something looked terribly wrong. "What exactly did you see when you found him?"

"Just as he is now, slumped over the writing desk. As though he just... stopped. But Ginny, it's all wrong. There are two teacups—one overturned beside his hand, the other sitting clean on the side table. And his papers..." She shuddered. "They're not just scattered like someone dropped them. They look deliberately searched through, with some pages missing entirely."

"Two teacups?" He hadn't been alone all night, then.

"Yes, and that's not the tea I brought this morning. That's on the counter in the kitchen. He had a visitor. Someone he was comfortable enough with to share tea." Her voice dropped to a whisper. "And the smell, Ginny. Like a cat's been in here and didn't have a litter box. I don't allow pets. So it must be something else."

A siren wailed in the distance, growing closer. Shirley's face crumpled with relief. "That'll be Dr. Westbrook. Thank heavens she was able to come quickly."

The siren stopped outside, followed by car doors slamming and urgent voices. Shirley hurried downstairs to let them in while I stayed by Tobias's door, fighting the urge to look more closely at what lay beyond.

"Morning, Ginny." Dr. Westbrook appeared at the top of the stairs, medical bag in hand, her usual cheerful demeanor replaced by professional concern. "Heard we might have a problem. I called PC Trewin to drive me over."

PC Trewin followed behind her, looking more serious than I'd ever seen the usually easygoing village policeman. "Mrs. Pengelly, you're the one who found him?"

"Yes, about twenty minutes ago. I brought his morning tea, but he…" Shirley's voice trailed off as she gestured helplessly toward the door.

Dr. Westbrook stepped inside the room. From where I stood, I could see more details now—Shirley was correct. The pages scattered around the room were in piles. Someone had been sifting through them, dropping the discards and pacing while they worked. Doing it all so quietly to avoid disturbing other guests. Perhaps the police would uncover whatever the searcher wanted.?

"Has anyone else been in here?" Dr. Westbrook asked.

"Just me, and only for a moment," Shirley said. "I checked for a pulse, but there wasn't one."

The examination took several tense minutes. Dr. Westbrook moved around the room, noting details that would help the police. When she finally emerged, her expression was grim.

"I'm afraid he's definitely gone. Been dead for at least four hours, possibly longer."

Shirley sank against the wall. "Oh, that poor man. What could have happened? He seemed perfectly healthy yesterday. A heart attack, or one of those aneurysms?"

"That's what concerns me," Dr. Westbrook said. "Constable Trewin, this needs to go to CID immediately. I can't be sure until the autopsy, but there's a smell. Foxglove leaves. This might be digitalis poisoning."

"Digitalis?" I asked.

"Foxglove," she explained. "No helpful signs, but that odor is what I recognized. If I'm right, someone added ground up foxglove to the tea. It will be important to preserve that evidence."

"Not a crime of passion, then," Constable Trewin said grimly. He pulled out his phone and called in the incident.

Dr. Westbrook nodded. "The interesting thing is, the visitor's cup is untouched. They didn't drink—just watched him take in the tainted tea. It's odd that your victim wouldn't wonder why two cups but only one brew."

The words settled over us like a cold fog. As PC Trewin observed, poisoning meant murder. Murder meant one of us —someone in our small community—was a killer.

PC Trewin stood in the doorway blocking my view. "I need you to bring all the guests to the kitchen, and join them to wait for DI Drake."

"The other guests are probably up now, the siren would have woken them," Shirley said taking control of the situation. "Ginny, could you inform them. I'll get a breakfast going. Oh your discussion? And your last walk. I'm so sorry this doesn't look good for the future of your tours."

I half hoped so. Oliver's idea had sounded like a good one. But now. I'd been regretting the choice to run them already, and now we had a murder.

"The walk's canceled," I said, my mind already moving to practical matters. "After DI Drake is done, perhaps I can bring the remaining guests to Hampton books. Give you time to sort out how to manage the extended stay."

"The extended stay? Oh, the police will want them to stay around, yes." She headed toward the kitchen muttering about registrations.

8

A n hour later, I found myself in the surreal position of serving tea and biscuits to a group of shocked literary tourists who were still reeling over the fact that their fellow participant had been murdered overnight. All the time wondering if one of them was doing a great acting job.

"I can't believe he's dead?" Dr. Sterling set down her teacup with a sharp clink. "I saw him just last night. He was perfectly fine."

"When was that?" I asked, settling behind the bookshop counter where I could observe everyone's reactions.

DI Drake had allowed us to relocate since she was busy with collecting clues and finding a location for an incident room. So her interviews had been postponed. I'm sure she would not appreciate me asking questions before she could speak to the potential suspects, but I couldn't ignore the situation. And I would tell her everything, so I wasn't being nosy, I was helping the police.

"After dinner. Around nine, perhaps? He was coming out of the dining room when I went upstairs." She shook her head in bewilderment. "He seemed a bit agitated, but not ill."

Lily Ashworth had chosen a chair by the window, her notebook already out, perhaps how she processed the shock. "What exactly happened to him?"

"The police aren't certain yet," I said carefully. "But the doctor suspects he was poisoned."

The word fell into silence like a stone into still water. Edmund Fitzmoore went pale, his coffee cup halfway to his lips.

"Poisoned?" Lily's pen hovered over her notebook. "I thought you were exaggerating when you said murder. But it could be an accident, or he took his own life?"

Fitzmoore set his cup down. "If it was an accidental poisoning, how did we survive? And do you think someone would really poison themselves. It's never an easy death. You should know that from your historical romances."

Dr. Sterling pressed her hands to her temples. "This is unbelievable. Who would want to hurt Tobias? He was just a writer researching his book."

"Was he, though?" Edmund asked, his voice tight with strain. "Because the questions he'd been asking didn't sound like research to me. They sounded like interrogation. And none of the answers were his business. Perhaps he annoyed a local into brewing up a nasty silencer."

I was shocked at his accusation, but before I could say anything, Beau stepped inside, stopping short when he saw the assembled group. "I thought you'd still be at the B&B. There are police outside. You all look serious. Everything alright?"

"Tobias Fletcher is dead," I said simply. "Murdered, apparently."

Beau's expression shifted instantly to crisis management mode. "When? How?"

"Sometime last night. Poisoned, the doctor thinks." I told him we didn't have any details other than sometime after nine pm and before six thirty am.

He moved to stand beside my chair, his presence comforting. "What do the police need?"

Before I could answer, the door opened again and Elliot entered, taking in the scene with a quick assessment. I hoped he didn't come to the wrong conclusion about Beau's proximity to me.

"Heard the sirens earlier," he said. "Shirley mentioned something had happened at the B&B."

I gave him the update, hoping that was the last time I'd have to repeat the details.

Elliot's expression grew grave. "What kind of symptoms? I've dealt with some of the animals in my care getting into all sorts of plants they shouldn't."

"He looked like he just died," I said. "Dr. Westbrook suggested foxglove."

"And there were two teacups in his room," I added. "Someone visited him last night."

Elliot frowned. "Plant-based poisons can produce very specific symptoms. If the police need botanical expertise..."

"They might," I said. "Detective Inspector Drake is on the job."

The mention of CID seemed to make everything more real. Edmund shifted nervously in his chair. "How long will we need to stay? I have publishing deadlines, business obligations..."

"Those will have to wait," Beau said with the authority of someone who'd managed plenty of corporate crises. "When police investigate a murder, everything else stops. Surely you have the ability to run your business remotely."

"Murder," Dr. Sterling repeated faintly. "I still can't believe it. Things like this don't happen to people like us."

"What do you mean, people like us?" Lily asked sharply.

"Well, we're just... ordinary people. Writers, academics. Not the sort who get mixed up in violence."

"Someone was mixed up in violence enough to kill him," Edmund pointed out. "The question is why."

An uncomfortable silence settled over the group. Malcolm appeared from the back room, carrying a tray with fresh tea and looking more composed than the rest of us.

"I've prepared additional refreshments," he announced. "Given the circumstances, it seemed appropriate to offer proper hospitality while we wait for the authorities."

"Thank you, Malcolm." I watched him set out fresh cups and saucers with his usual precision, grateful for his steadying presence. "What's your take on all this?"

Malcolm straightened, considering his words carefully. "Mr. Fletcher exhibited behavior consistent with investigation rather than literary research. His questions were too specific, too personal. Someone conducting that level of inquiry often discovers information others prefer to keep private."

"You think he found out something that got him killed?" Dr. Sterling asked.

"I think," Malcolm said, choosing his words with care, "that Mr. Fletcher was preparing to confront someone. Yesterday evening, he asked me quite pointed questions about discretion and professional ethics. He also mentioned having made an appointment for this morning—something about settling matters properly."

This was news to all of us. Edmund's coffee cup rattled against its saucer as he set it down.

"An appointment with whom?" Lily asked.

"He didn't specify, but he seemed... triumphant about it. As if he held some advantage."

The front door opened once more, this time admitting a woman with graying hair and intelligent eyes. She surveyed our group with professional assessment before focusing on me.

"Miss Hampton? We seem to meet over bodies more frequently than most people."

"Yes, of course. These are the other tour participants—Dr. Sterling, Ms. Ashworth, and Mr. Fitzmoore." I gestured to each in turn. "And Malcolm, who works with me here in the bookshop. You might not remember Dr. Harrington, the local veterinarian, and my friend Beau Morrison from America."

"I do remember you," DI Drake said, nodding to everyone before addressing the group. "I understand Mr. Fletcher was part of your literary tour. I'll need to speak with each of you individually, but first I want to establish a timeline. When did you last see Mr. Fletcher alive?"

"Around nine last night," Dr. Sterling said. "He was leaving the dining room when I went upstairs."

"He seemed upset about something," Edmund added. "Kept checking his phone and muttering."

"What about after nine o'clock? Did anyone hear or see anything unusual?"

Lily raised her hand tentatively. "I heard someone walking in the corridor quite late. After midnight, I think. I wouldn't swear it was Tobias, but it might have been." Her eyes widened. "Oh my goodness. It could have been the killer. I'm glad I didn't look. And I suppose I'm a little disappointed at the same time. It would have helped to know their identity."

"That might have been me," Edmund said. "I couldn't sleep, so I went down to the kitchen for water. Mrs. Pengelly said it was fine to help myself."

DI Drake nodded and made a note. "Did you see anyone else during this late-night excursion?"

Edmund looked at the ceiling for a moment while he considered the question. "No, but I thought I heard voices from one of the rooms. Muffled conversation. Possibly Fletcher's place."

DI Drake continued to make notes, her expression revealing nothing. "Mr. Fletcher had been asking questions about people's professional backgrounds, I understand? Inappropriate questions."

The group exchanged glances. Finally, Dr. Sterling spoke up. "He seemed very interested in our credentials. Asked specific questions about my Oxford research and yes, I took some offense and he didn't justify his curiosity to my satisfaction. Not a motive for murder. I assure you."

"He knew details about my business that he shouldn't have had access to," Edmund added nervously. "Financial records, client information. When I asked how he'd obtained it, he just smiled and said he had excellent research skills."

"He photographed Mrs. Pengelly's guest registry yesterday," Lily added. "Claimed it was for research, but that made no sense."

DI Drake's pen moved steadily. "I've just come from the crime scene. The evidence suggests Mr. Fletcher was expecting his visitor—no indication that someone forced their way in. The teacups indicate he was comfortable with the killer. He had documents out, possibly to share."

"What kind of documents?" Dr. Sterling asked.

"His manuscript pages show evidence of being sorted into specific piles before being searched through. Some pages are missing entirely—removed deliberately, not scattered randomly." DI Drake's gaze moved across the group. "The victim's phone shows several outgoing calls yesterday evening, including one at 11:15 PM that lasted only thirty seconds."

Edmund had gone pale. "Thirty seconds? That isn't very long."

"Just long enough to confirm an appointment, wouldn't you say?" DI Drake observed. "Someone he'd been expecting. Someone who came prepared with foxglove extract and left. Perhaps while Mr. Fletcher was still conscious."

The clinical details made the crime feel both more real and more chilling. Her words removed any suggestion this was an accident. It was calculated, deliberate murder.

The implications hung heavy in the morning air. The most probably suspects sat in this room. Someone with a secret dark enough to justify murder. The cozy literary tour had become something far more sinister.

"I'll be conducting formal interviews this afternoon," DI Drake continued. "Until then, I need everyone to remain in Tidehaven Cove and available for questioning. This is now a murder investigation."

"Where are we supposed to stay?" Edmund asked. "We were supposed to checkout."

"Mrs. Pengelly has arranged for you to stay in your rooms at the B&B. I don't expect this to take more than a few days."

"And how do we know someone else won't die?" Lily asked in a sharp tone I hadn't expected.

DI Drake snapped her notebook closed. "I'm sure you'll

be as safe there as anywhere else. As I said, I intend to solve this case quickly."

As she prepared to leave, she turned back to address me specifically. "Miss Hampton, given your previous experience and your role organizing this tour, I'd appreciate your assistance with community liaison. But no amateur investigation this time—this is too dangerous."

After she left, an uncomfortable silence settled over the bookshop. The tour participants sat scattered among the reading chairs, avoiding each other's eyes. Whatever secrets they'd brought to Devon, one of them had proven deadly.

"I suppose this is the end of our literary tour," Dr. Sterling said eventually, her voice small.

"Rather dramatically ended," Malcolm observed, beginning to clear the untouched tea service.

Edmund stood abruptly. "I should call my office, explain why I'll be delayed."

"Sit down," Lily said sharply. "We're all suspects now. Running off to make private phone calls won't look good."

"I'm not running off," Edmund protested, but he remained standing, agitated energy radiating from him like heat. "I have a business to run."

Beau moved closer to my chair. "This is a crisis management situation now. Everyone needs to stay calm and follow police procedures."

"Easy for you to say," Edmund snapped. "You're not the one with business deadlines and clients expecting—"

"Edmund." Dr. Sterling's voice cut through his rising panic. "Stop. You're making yourself look guilty."

The words hung in the air like an accusation. Edmund's face flushed red, then drained of color entirely.

"I'm not guilty of anything," he said, but his voice lacked conviction.

Outside, the morning mist was lifting from the harbor, revealing what should have been a beautiful day. Fishing boats bobbed peacefully at their moorings, and early tourists were beginning to wander the village streets, unaware that murder had visited Tidehaven Cove in the night.

Austen and Hardy had positioned themselves strategically around the room, and both dogs continued watching Edmund with unusual intensity. Their instincts had been helpful before—I'd have to pay attention to what they were trying to tell me.

"Well," I said, trying to inject a little normalcy into the situation, "we might as well make ourselves comfortable. It looks like we'll be here for a while."

But comfortable was the last thing any of us felt. Someone in this room had poured deadly tea for Tobias Fletcher last night. It's possible they stayed and watched him die. Someone with secrets dark enough to kill for.

The cozy literary tour had become something far more dangerous, and the killer was still among us, sitting in my bookshop, drinking Malcolm's perfectly prepared tea, and pretending to be as shocked as the rest of us.

9

"Ginny, dear, you look absolutely dreadful." Elspeth arrived at Hampton's Books later that day carrying a tray laden with enough biscuits and cakes to feed half the village. "Dot and I thought you might need proper sustenance during this terrible business."

Behind her, Dot Jenkins bustled in with arms full of fresh flowers. "Can't have our bookshop looking gloomy when there's investigating to be done," she announced, immediately beginning to arrange daffodils around the shop.

Through the front window, I could see the yellow police tape fluttering around Shirley's B&B like garish party streamers. The village hall across the green had been transformed into a temporary police station, with constables trudging back and forth carrying evidence boxes.

"Dr. Sterling was in there for nearly two hours," I told them, accepting a cup of tea gratefully. "When she came out, she looked like she'd seen a ghost."

Austen and Hardy positioned themselves near Elspeth's

cake tray, employing their most effective begging expressions. Hardy's tail wagged hopefully while Austen maintained the dignity befitting her literary namesake—though
her nose twitched at the scent of lemon drizzle.

"Well, I can't say I'm surprised," Dot said, though her
tone carried more concern than satisfaction. "That woman
knows more about poisonous plants than anyone has a right
to. Yesterday she was asking very specific questions about
my foxglove."

"What kind of questions?" I asked, suddenly alert. Was
this revelation why DI Drake had kept questioning her?

"Technical ones. Which parts of the plant contain the
highest concentration of digitalis, historical extraction
methods, dosage calculations for therapeutic versus lethal
effects." Dot paused meaningfully. "She even asked about
Victorian-era preparation techniques—claimed it was for
her research on period mystery novels. I'm not a chemist, I
told her."

My stomach dropped. "That's quite detailed."

"Oh, it wasn't just asking. She knew things that would
make a pharmacist nervous," Elspeth added. "When I
mentioned using foxglove tea for heart palpitations like my
grandmother did, Dr. Sterling went white as a sheet. Started
lecturing about how many Victorian ladies died from
improper dosing. I suppose that's her area of expertise, but
why was she asking me for information?"

Interesting that Dr. Sterling hadn't mentioned any of this
during our talks.

"She said the literary world was full of accurate poison
information because mystery writers research thoroughly,"
Dot continued. "But honestly, Ginny, she sounded more like
a botanist than someone with a doctorate in literature."

The efficient village gossip network never ceased to

amaze me. Information traveled faster through Tidehaven Cove than through any modern communication system— and it was usually disturbingly accurate.

"Mrs. Pengelly mentioned the police found foxglove residue in poor Mr. Fletcher's teacup," Elspeth said gravely. "Digitalis poisoning, according to Dr. Westbrook's preliminary examination. Though you know that, Ginny."

I felt like I was being reprimanded for not feeding the grapevine. "How do you know that?" I asked.

"Dr. Westbrook's receptionist is my niece," Elspeth said matter-of-factly. "She overheard her discussing the symptoms with the police. Sent off samples for testing. The poor man would have been going crazy before he died."

The bell chimed as Dr. Sterling returned from her interrogation, looking not just pale but genuinely shaken. She practically collapsed into one of the reading chairs, her usual composed academic demeanor completely absent.

"They think I murdered him," she said without preamble, her voice barely above a whisper. "My botanical expertise, my..." She stopped, glancing around the room with obvious distress.

"My what?" Elspeth prompted gently, settling beside her with maternal concern. "Just because you know how, doesn't mean you killed the poor man."

"My academic credentials," Dr. Sterling whispered, then looked up with obvious panic. "But that's not why they suspect me. Like you said Mr. Willoughby, I know the exact dosage that would be required. I'm a bit of an expert on these things. Thanks to the Victorians and their penchant for poisoning."

"What do you mean?" I asked.

"When Detective Inspector Drake described the crime scene, I blurted out the technique I knew from my Victorian literature research. Foxglove leaves steeped in hot tea for precisely eight minutes, then the plant matter removed to avoid obvious detection. It's described in several 19th-century mystery novels, including cases based on real poisoning trials."

The room went very quiet.

"I told them about the historical precedents—how Victorian ladies used digitalis tea for heart ailments but frequently miscalculated dosages, how mystery writers of the period documented the exact symptoms... How in those days there was no test for poisoning, so killers mostly went free." She pressed her hands to her face. "I was trying to be helpful, but I realized I was describing the perfect murder method. What a fool I am."

Before anyone could respond, the door burst open and Lily tumbled in, followed by Edmund who looked like he'd rather be anywhere else on earth. Behind them came Beau, carrying his laptop.

"They're questioning everyone again!" Lily announced breathlessly. "They've found something disturbing in Tobias's room. It's going to be the bare light bulb and yelling version this time."

"Don't be ridiculous," Dr. Sterling said, recovering some of her equilibrium. "This isn't a novel. It's real life. That kind of behavior will get any case thrown out."

Beau set his laptop on the nearest table and opened it with purpose. "The police showed me some of his portfolio contents. They asked me for help because of my publishing industry experience, I can tell you we're dealing with something much more serious than a frustrated writer."

"What do you mean?" I asked. Tobias Fletcher wasn't a publisher.

"Mr. Fletcher was running a sophisticated investigation

operation. His portfolio contained multiple writing samples of vastly different quality levels—some genuine literary work, others amateur attempts to disguise plagiarism. He also had records from a publishing house."

"Mine. He said he was doing research on some corporate espionage and needed to research how that might work. I sanitized a few months of data and sent it to him." Edmund slumped into a chair, his usual nervous energy replaced by defeated exhaustion. "His thriller writing must have affected his mind. What would have happened if he submitted it for publishing? The man was convinced people were lying about everything."

"The quality of his analysis is fascinating," Beau continued, pulling up a detailed spreadsheet. "I've seen this pattern before in publishing fraud cases. High-quality original work systematically degraded by adding inferior material to throw off plagiarism detection software."

Elspeth poured tea. "But he carried that portfolio everywhere. Guarded it like the crown jewels."

"Because it contained something far more valuable than his own writing," Beau said grimly. "Something most people in the industry would ignore but he thought was criminal. A persistent falsification of facts and people trading on credentials they didn't possess."

"You mean he was investigating academic fraud?" Dr. Sterling asked, her voice barely audible.

"More than investigating," Beau replied. "He was cataloging it for leverage. I found reference files on at least a dozen people. Publishers, academics, tour guides, even literary agents. Financial records, background verification attempts, copies of disputed credentials."

Malcolm joined us from the back room, his timing impeccable as always. "Perhaps this would be an appropriate moment to mention that I overheard portions of Mr. Fletcher's phone conversation last evening."

"What phone conversation?" I asked sharply. Why did Malcolm hold information back?

"Around seven o'clock, I was locking up when I heard raised voices from across the green. Mr. Fletcher was just outside Mrs. Pengelly's garden, speaking quite heatedly to someone about final deadlines and consequences for non-cooperation. They were quite loud. I'd be very surprised if I was the only one who witnessed it."

Edmund had gone pale. "He called me just after seven. Said he'd found irregularities in my business registration and client verification processes."

"What kind of irregularities?" I asked.

"Serious fact checking errors. Questions about whether certain manuscripts I'd published actually belonged to the credited authors." Edmund's voice was barely audible. "He was right—some of my clients have been... less than honest about how much creativity they'd added to their creative non-fiction."

"Did you meet with him?" Beau asked. "Did you tell the police?"

"No! I hung up immediately. Told him I wouldn't discuss my business with a stranger." Edmund had the grace to look ashamed when he said, "I didn't think it had anything to do with his death. So, no the police don't have that little bit of evidence."

"But someone did meet with him," I said, thinking aloud. "Mrs. Pengelly heard voices around midnight. Two teacups in his room."

DI Drake's voice came from the doorway. "Which brings us to some interesting discoveries about Mr. Fletcher's true activities."

She'd entered so quietly none of us had noticed. Behind her came a constable carrying several evidence bags.

"We've completed our initial analysis of the victim's portfolio contents," she announced, surveying our impromptu gathering. "Mr. Morrison's publishing expertise has been invaluable in understanding what we're dealing with. Though I had hoped he wouldn't rush over and tell everyone."

She produced a manila folder and spread several documents on the nearest table. "Mr. Fletcher wasn't writing fiction. He was documenting reality—specifically, a network of credential fraud and plagiarism in the literary world."

I leaned forward and felt my heart sink. Background checks, financial records, academic verification requests—all meticulously organized by target.

"He was blackmailing people," Lily said, her voice flat.

"Systematically," DI Drake confirmed. "Dr. Sterling, your file contains inquiries to Oxford University about your claimed PhD, copies of tour company applications listing false credentials, even photographs of you conducting educational tours under fraudulent academic authority."

Dr. Sterling's composure finally cracked completely. "I never claimed to be something I wasn't intellectually. My knowledge is genuine—years of independent research, authentic expertise. But without formal credentials..."

"The academic world won't take you seriously," I finished gently.

"Exactly. So I... embellished my qualifications to get work. Tour guide positions, freelance research projects, literary consulting." She wiped her eyes. "It started small but became easier to elaborate as people believed me. I never falsified my research, though."

"And Mr. Fletcher discovered this?" DI Drake asked.

"Tuesday evening. He showed me his documentation—proof of every false assumption I'd ever allowed people to make. He wanted me to provide academic endorsement for his manuscript in exchange for keeping quiet. He wasn't writing anything that needed my stamp of approval."

"But here's what's interesting," Beau interjected, studying the evidence spread across the table. "In these few pages of his manuscript I can see clear signs of someone else's voice."

DI Drake nodded. "We believe Mr. Fletcher was committing the very sins he used as blackmail fodder. As though he'd taken the position that if you can't beat them, exploit them. Nothing he has here is criminal. I'm sure that led to his actions if no police department took his case."

"Is the literary world so riddled with corruption?" Dot asked.

Beau shook his head. "No more than any other industry."

"Enough that this gives several people compelling motive for murder," DI Drake observed.

10

"Perhaps," I suggested, "we should all be very honest about our whereabouts last night. Starting with everyone's actual movements after dinner."

DI Drake didn't seem to mind me leading the discussion. Surely she'd asked each of the tour attendees the same question. Instead of ordering me to stay out of the investigation, she turned her attention to Lily, who had been taking extensive notes throughout our discussion. "Ms. Ashworth, you've been documenting our conversation quite thoroughly. Professional habit? Are you not a Romance writer?"

Lily looked up from her notebook, startled. "I... yes, I suppose. Writers observe everything. I'm considering a new pen name and a foray into romantic crime fiction."

Beau glanced at her pages. "Those aren't casual observations—that's highly detailed information gathering. Interview-style questioning, source verification notes..."

Lily's pause was telling. "I'm... thorough in my research."

Whatever she was, a good liar under attention was not it. "What kind of research exactly?" I asked, studying her defensive posture.

She waved her hand dismissively, her bracelet's clacking. "I told you. I'm thinking of writing crime fiction. This is a valuable opportunity to get details right."

"Ms. Ashworth," DI Drake interrupted, "we found your business cards in Mr. Fletcher's portfolio. Not romance writer business cards. Investigative journalism cards."

The revelation hit like a bomb. Edmund's teacup clattered against its saucer.

I thought back over the last few days, remembering her questions and attitude. I should have realized, my only excuse was that unlike Tobias, I was taking everyone at face value.

"You're a journalist?" Dr. Sterling asked, her voice barely a whisper.

Lily stood and tossed her notebook on the table. "Fine. Yes, I'm an investigative journalist—freelance of course like everyone in my field these days," Lily corrected, abandoning her pretense. "I was researching this kind of fraud for a series on academic and publishing industry corruption. Tobias Fletcher wasn't my target—he was my competition. My romance books don't pay the bills."

She knew more about Tobias than she'd let on.

"Competition how?" I asked.

"We were both investigating the same network of fraudulent credentials and publishing scams. But he was using his research for blackmail while I was building a legitimate news story."

"Did you find anything that would lead us to the killer?" Beau asked. "Since you kept relevant facts from the police, how do we know we can trust you?"

DI Drake spoke before Lily could answer Beau. "And you knew Tobias was a fraud from the beginning. Is that right? Did you intend on exposing his blackmail scheme?"

"I suspected. His story about being a political thriller writer never aligned with his actual writing activities. When I heard his research questions during the tour, I recognized investigative techniques. He wasn't professional, but there are only a few ways to gather facts."

"Why didn't you expose him?" Elspeth asked. "You put us all in danger. Just for a headline."

"I didn't know he'd be killed. I kept quiet because I needed to understand the scope of his operation first. How many people he was targeting, what evidence he'd gathered, how the blackmail network functioned." Lily's voice carried professional frustration. "If I'd acted too quickly, all his victims would have remained vulnerable, and I would have lost a lucrative story."

"And last night?" DI Drake asked.

Lily's pause stretched uncomfortably long. "He called around eleven. Said he knew who I really was and wanted to make a deal. Claimed he had evidence that would make my story irrelevant because everyone involved would be too compromised to publish."

DI Drake checked that PC Trewin was taking notes. "Did you meet with him?"

"Blackmail only works if two things are in place. The truth is provable and the victim is terrified of the result of saying no." Another pause. "I went to his room around eleven-thirty. But when I got there..." She stopped, pressing her lips together.

"What happened?" Dot asked. It was hard to ignore her grandmotherly concern.

"The door was already open. He was on the floor, and there was a terrible smell like urine."

"And you didn't call for help?" Edmund asked, his voice tight with anxiety.

"He was already dead. I panicked. If anyone discovered an investigative journalist at the scene of a murder involving blackmail..." She looked around the room helplessly. "My story would be killed, my career destroyed. All those people he was blackmailing would never get justice."

"So you took his portfolio," I said, understanding dawning.

"As much as I could grab fast. I thought I could still write the article, reveal the corruption properly instead of letting it die with him." She spread her hands in front of her. "You have what I left behind."

"Withholding evidence is a serious crime, Ms. Ashworth. Where is it now?" DI Drake asked sharply.

"Hidden in my room at the B&B. I was planning to turn it over once I'd photographed everything. I needed the proof too."

The admission hung heavy in the air. But something still bothered me—a detail that didn't fit.

"Lily," I said, "if Tobias was already dead when you arrived, did you move his body? Because Mrs. Pengelly found him sitting upright at the desk this morning."

Her face went white. "He was on the floor face down when I found him. I didn't even check his pulse. I knew there was no hope."

Which meant someone else had been in that room after Lily left. Someone who'd positioned the body, arranged the scene.

Austen gave a genteel woof and Hardy rubbed against my leg. There was something they thought we were missing. Both turned to stare at Edmund.

"Edmund," I said, "the dogs have been watching you all afternoon. In my experience, they usually have good reasons."

Edmund's face crumpled with relief. It seemed he also had a secret. "You want the truth? Fine. I didn't hang up on Tobias last night."

"What did happen?" DI Drake asked.

"He had documentation of everything. Client contracts where I'd published work with unconfirmed facts. False authorship, authentication certificates, ones I'd forged for rare manuscripts." Edmund's voice broke slightly. "My business was finished if that information became public."

"So you agreed to cooperate?" Beau asked.

"He wanted me to authenticate his manuscripts using my credentials." Edmund looked around the room with haunted eyes. "I said I needed time to consider his proposal."

"But you met with him anyway," I said.

"Around midnight. I went to tell him I couldn't do it— that I'd rather lose my business than become part of his fraud network."

"And?" DI Drake prompted.

"He was already dead when I arrived. Exactly like Lily described."

"So you both discovered the body and neither of you called the police?" I asked.

"I got there after Lily," Edmund said quietly. "Found him around eleven-forty-five. There were documents under his body. I checked to see if any had my name, but they didn't. I tossed them around and then repositioning him."

"Why did you move the body?" DI Drake asked sharply.

Edmund's answer came out in a whisper. "I found one of my letterheads with our agreement to his terms. Under his body where you could have found it. His body was clearly moved when I was done, so posing it seemed a good move."

"DI Drake isn't one to arrest someone without solid

proof," I said. "Did you think you would get away with interfering with a crime scene?"

"I didn't know what the police would do. So I took the letter and arranged him in a writing position to suggest he'd been working alone when he died. I thought... I thought it might look like natural causes or suicide."

"And the teacups?" DI Drake asked.

"What teacups?" His genuine confusion was obvious to everyone in the room.

"Two teacups on the desk. He was entertaining someone and that's how he was poisoned."

"No. There were only papers. Please believe me, I didn't... I wouldn't..." Edmund looked around the room desperately. "I just took the letter and left. I swear that's all I did."

"Which means," I said slowly, "someone else visited that room after both Lily and Edmund had been there. Someone who might have known about Dr. Sterling's botanical expertise and wanted to frame her."

The implication settled over us like a chill. We weren't dealing with a crime of passion or desperation—this was calculated murder with deliberate misdirection.

"The question becomes," DI Drake said, "who knew enough about everyone's secrets to plan such an elaborate frame-up?"

Austen suddenly stood and walked to the window, her body tense with alertness. Hardy joined her, both dogs staring intently at something outside.

"Someone's watching us," I said, moving to join them.

Through the glass, I could see a figure standing in the shadow of the teashop. Too far away to identify, but clearly focused on the bookshop.

Malcolm coughed gently and said, "I noticed earlier but thought it might be a tourist."

As we watched, the figure melted back into the shadows and disappeared.

"Right," I said, feeling the familiar rush of determination that came with a mystery finally starting to make sense. "Here's what we know: Tobias was murdered by someone with botanical knowledge, but we don't know if that was Dr. Sterling. Lily and Edmund both discovered the body but claim they didn't kill him. Someone else staged the scene to point us at Dr. Sterling. We don't know if any of the evidence is staged or real."

"My investigation, Ginny," DI Drake said.

"Someone who knew all our secrets," Dr. Sterling said quietly, totally ignoring the DI.

"But who?" Lily asked. "Who else knew about Tobias's blackmail operation?"

"That," I said, "is what we need to figure out. Because whoever killed Tobias Fletcher is still out there, and they're clever enough to frame innocent people."

DI Drake checked her watch. "I'll need new written statements from everyone about your movements last night —complete honesty this time. And Ms. Ashworth, that portfolio needs to be in police custody immediately."

"Of course," Lily said. "I'll get it right now."

"Dot," DI Drake continued, "I'll need you to compile a list of everyone in the village with enough botanical knowledge to have committed this crime."

"That's... quite a few people, actually," Dot said thoughtfully. "The gardening club, anyone who's taken horticultural courses, retired pharmacists, even amateur mystery writers who research poisons."

"Then we'll interview them all," DI Drake said firmly. "I know you all want to help, for various reasons. But leave this to the police. We will get answers."

DI Drake ordered Dr. Sterling and Edmund to report to the incident room and left with Lily to retrieve the portfolio. When they were gone, the remaining group sat in contemplative silence. The comfortable bookshop atmosphere felt charged with new possibilities—and new dangers.

"Well," Elspeth announced, beginning to clear teacups with renewed purpose, "this calls for a proper village response. Can't have clever murderers running about Tidehaven Cove thinking they've outwitted us."

"What kind of response?" I asked, though I suspected I'd regret the question.

"Information sharing, of course. Dot can coordinate with the gardening club—anyone showing unusual interest in poisonous plants. Mrs. Pengelly can monitor our suspects. I'll handle tea shop intelligence. Before we find the killer, we need to prove Tidehaven is innocent of this crime."

It was like watching her organize the village's own counterintelligence operation. I found myself torn between admiration and concern for their safety.

"The thing is," I said, "we're dealing with someone who's been several steps ahead of us from the beginning. They knew about Tobias's blackmail operation, they knew about Dr. Sterling's botanical expertise, they even knew enough to make Edmund and Lily look suspicious."

"Someone with access to inside information," Beau said thoughtfully. "Publishing industry connections, academic networks..."

"Certainly not someone who lives here," I said. "No motive."

"Most likely one of your tour people," Dot said. "We'll find them, don't you worry."

11

The police station—normally village hall—felt cramped with the weight of Tobias Fletcher's deception spread across three tables. DI Drake had organized the portfolio contents into distinct categories, and the contrast was striking.

"Look at this progression," DI Drake said, gesturing to the arranged manuscripts. "These early pieces are barely coherent—he's forming his understanding of the plot he believes exists. But then we have this." She held up a polished manuscript page. "Well documented facts, proof—at least what he saw as proof of his suspicions."

I examined the work closely. "Are we sure this isn't two people? I can't imagine the author went from barely able to form a sentence to assembling a coherent documentation of fraud. At first glance at least."

Beau pulled out his tablet and opened a spreadsheet he'd been building. "I ran a few pages of the manuscript through a plagiarism checker. They're not all that accurate but the results are showing this as about fifty percent copied. The report on phrasing and grammar used hints that Ginny is right."

"Ghostwriting arrangements?" DI Drake asked. "I know they're quite common in things like celebrity books, not just biographies, but could he have engaged someone to create the final documents?"

"It's possible," Beau replied, consulting his data. "Ghost-writers usually maintain consistent style to avoid detection, but if they didn't see the first drafts, a writer for hire might not know how different it was. These do read like stolen submissions or plagiarized work from different authors, but they could be samples from conspiracy sites. I mean there are multiple ones of those for every flavor of paranoia."

DI Drake moved to a second table covered with financial documents. "We may never know. We have information we can verify here—bank statements showing irregular deposits, always in cash, ranging from £500 to £3,000. Payment schedules that may be blackmail. And this..." She held up a ledger. "Client tracking with initials, amounts owed, and what he calls leverage levels. I've seen this before, bookies use these systems."

I studied the ledger entries. "R.S. - £2,000 monthly - Level 3. E.H. - £1,500 quarterly - Level 4. L.A. - £800 monthly - Level 2. These aren't just the tour participants—there are dozens of entries."

"The fact he was being paid is concerning. It means his research turned up true crimes," Beau said. "He's got academic verification documents, employment history fabrications, and what looks like stolen submissions from multiple literary journals. Look at these email threads—he's been contacting universities, publishers, and literary magazines posing as a fact-checker."

A third table held correspondence that worried me even

more. DI Drake picked up a folder labeled Active Negotiations. "Reviewing subject's credentials for accuracy—that's blackmail initiation, I'm fairly sure. Monthly consultation fees for discretion services—that's payment demands. Historical discrepancies requiring ongoing confidentiality—that's the ongoing threat."

"These submission deadlines," Beau said, scanning the documents with his publisher's eye. "I recognize some of these literary magazines and academic journals. He's been targeting people during crucial career moments—grant applications, tenure reviews, major publication opportunities. The psychological pressure on his victims must have been immense."

I read over his shoulder, feeling lightheaded with the scope of the scheme. "'Your Oxford credentials require clarification before the Whitmore Prize committee reviews your submission.' He wasn't just stealing money—he was torturing people with the constant threat of exposure."

"And it was highly profitable torture," DI Drake added grimly. "Financial records suggest £15,000-20,000 monthly from active victims. This wasn't opportunistic blackmail—it was his primary income source."

"The systematic nature is what's most disturbing," Beau said, creating categories on his tablet. "Academic fraud, literary theft, credential verification scams—he had multiple revenue streams all targeting the same community vulnerabilities. And if it wasn't about ransoming people's reputations, he'd be a solid businessman. I hate to say it, but a lot of people fudge their resumes, and not just in publishing."

The door opened, and PC Trewin entered looking slightly overwhelmed. "Ma'am, Mrs. Pengelly's called three times in the last hour. Says she's remembered more details about the night of the murder, and she's made a proper tea if you'd like to come round. Refuses to talk to anyone but the boss."

Beau's phone buzzed insistently, and I watched his attention fragment. "Crisis at the office," he murmured, checking the message. "Printing deadline emergency that could affect our entire autumn distribution schedule."

"Can it wait?" DI Drake asked pointedly.

"Unfortunately, publishing schedules are unforgiving. This affects contracts worth millions and distribution agreements across Europe." He was already gathering his analysis materials. "But I've documented the manuscript findings— multiple authors, systematic theft, industrial-scale fraud. The evidence patterns are clear."

As he prepared to leave, Beau turned to me. "I'm sorry, but you know how it goes. You should think about your security. Someone might believe you know too much."

"That seems a bit much," I said, recognizing his instinct to treat my safety like a business crisis requiring professional management. "We're all perfectly safe. I have Austen and Hardy. And Malcolm and Freya if it comes to that. I'll make sure not to eat or drink anything from strangers."

"It's not a joke, Ginny. I can only hope you're right," he said over his shoulder as he left the tent.

DI Drake cleared her throat. "Right then. Mrs. Pengelly's and tea it is. Miss Hampton, do you think we can continue the investigation without business interruptions?"

Twenty minutes later, I sat on an overstuffed chair in Mrs. Pengelly's cozy sitting room, balancing delicate china while Austen and Hardy sprawled by the fireplace, thoroughly spoiled with homemade biscuits. The contrast between the clinical evidence room and this warm domestic space felt like emerging from a cave into sunlight.

"Two distinct voices in Mr. Fletcher's room," Mrs. Pengelly was saying, refilling teacups. "His voice was demanding, almost businesslike. The terms haven't changed, he kept saying. But the other person—they sounded desperate. Please, you don't understand what this will do to my career. There has to be another way."

"What time did this conversation occur?" DI Drake asked, her notebook balanced on her knee.

"Eleven-forty exactly. I always check the grandfather clock before my evening cocoa ritual." Mrs. Pengelly's eyes sparkled with satisfaction that she was being taken seriously. "The arguing went on for quite a while."

"Could you make out any other words?" I asked.

"Oh, yes. The visitor mentioned something about credentials being verified and publication deadlines. Mr. Fletcher kept referring to monthly arrangements and discretion fees. Most unpleasant business conversation, really."

DI Drake leaned forward. "Anything else? Footsteps, door openings? Was the other visitor a woman or a man?"

"Well, I have to say the voice was deep and I didn't recognize it. Neither of the ladies staying here sound at all like what I heard. After that visitor left, someone else came. Different footsteps entirely, much more confident. I heard the door open and close again around two in the morning. Whoever it was didn't stay long, perhaps fifteen minutes. I'm a light sleeper, you see."

"Two different visitors," I realized. "One being blackmailed, another with different business entirely."

"How is it you only remember these details now?" DI Drake asked.

Mrs. Pengelly looked down at her teacup. I was glad she

seemed to have some remorse for holding back and made a mental note never to stay in her B&B. I wouldn't sleep for worrying I was being watched.

"I didn't like to say in front of my guests. I didn't keep it secret, I think what they told you jogged my memory." She lifted the teapot. "Can I give you a top up?"

Before anyone could respond, there was a gentle knock at the front door. Mrs. Pengelly bustled out to greet the visitor, returning with Elliot, who carried his veterinary bag and looked slightly concerned.

"Sorry to interrupt," he said, "but Malcolm mentioned the dogs were here. I wanted to check Hardy's paw after yesterday's adventure—he seemed to be favoring it slightly during your walk."

Hardy immediately perked up at Elliot's voice, tail wagging as he approached for examination. Austen, not to be outdone, presented herself for attention as well.

"Nothing serious," Elliot pronounced after gentle examination. "Just a small pebble lodged between his pads. There we go, boy." Hardy licked his hand gratefully, accepting the treat offered.

"How thoughtful of you to check," Mrs. Pengelly beamed. "I do appreciate people who notice the small things. Will you join us for tea, Dr. Harrington?"

"Lovely," Elliot said, pulling a chair closer to the group.

"There's something else," Mrs. Pengelly added thoughtfully. "Mr. Fletcher had a visitor yesterday afternoon—before the evening confrontation. A young man, down from London, asking about the tour. I remember thinking he didn't seem like the type to be in the publishing business. His accent reminded me of that film, Snatch. You know what I mean. Not that the accent means he's a thug, but it just reminded me of those thugs. Not that lovely Brad Pitt, but the others."

"Could you give me a physical description of this visitor?" DI Drake asked ignoring the rambling.

"Medium height but seemed a bigger personality. Like I said, a bit of a gangster. He didn't say much in my hearing, but Mr. Fletcher definitely seemed afraid."

I tried to imagine the scene. "It sounds like our victim was stepping on some toes. Perhaps blackmailing the wrong person?"

DI Drake nodded at me. "The criminal world is small, and Fletcher wouldn't know if he was going after someone's cousin, or sibling. It's definitely something to investigate."

"I'm happy to do one of those drawing things," she said. "Oh that will be a good story to tell at the next book club."

12

"Mrs. Pengelly's testimony was very helpful," DI Drake said as we left the B&B. "We'll need to contact the gang special crimes unit in London. Maybe they'll know if one of the families has taken up publishing."

"We've been talking about village safety," Elliot said. "The village is setting up informal watch schedules. It seems Tidehaven might be attracting the wrong people. We'll keep an eye on the bookshop and Ginny, I think you should be escorted when you go from home to work."

DI Drake approved the plan over my objections—I couldn't be in danger for simply organizing a tour. Although it would have been nice if Oliver had taken his share of the work, so I'd have some time to think. Being part of the investigation and still trying to salvage something of the tour as planned was taking over my life. Freya was away in London visiting a few university friends. And the two men in my life were treating me so differently it made me wonder what was best. I could move into the apartment above the bookshop until Freya returned, but that felt like cowardice. And if I was in danger, how would the apartment be any safer than the cottage?

One thing I could start working on right now was my relationships. Beau's surprise visit was welcome in a way, but he clearly still put work ahead of me. Yes, deadlines existed, and crises happened, but it felt like that's all he'd done since arriving.

Elliott touched my arm, bringing me out of my head. "This is all a lot. How are you holding up with all this?"

"Better than I expected, actually." I watched Hardy investigate interesting scents while Austen stuck close to me and Elliot. "I suppose I can let DI Drake take the investigation, but she'd including me and I'm afraid of letting her down. This is my home now, and I'm responsible for the people who live in Tidehaven. I suppose, I don't like leaving things half done either. I do think I've been a help in figuring some things out."

"You are helping." He linked his arm in mine as we strolled the village green. "Is leaving things half done only about the investigation, or about life in general?"

"Both, really. Beau's a good person, but he sees everything as a problem to be solved rather than a situation to navigate together. I used to think that was what I needed— someone work beside me. To help me take charge and fix things."

He didn't defend his place in my life, just prompted me. "And now?"

"Now I realize I don't need help fixing things, and in reflection, I wonder how much was help and how much managing me. I've built something real here, and I'm quite capable of protecting it myself. With help from friends, of course." I thought about saying how I felt Beau wasn't paying me enough attention, but it sounded petty in my ears. And it was wrong to complain about one potential boyfriend to another—boyfriend didn't sound right, but nothing better came to mind.

Elliot gave my arm a squeeze. "I don't know how to help you with that, but I've been thinking about the foxglove poisoning. The knowledge required to use it effectively suggests someone with botanical or medical background. Or someone who's done very specific research."

It didn't narrow the suspect list. "Unfortunately, the internet provides everything one needs. And any good gardener will know the properties of their plants. Perhaps not how to turn them into a weapon, but how to be safe around them. What kind of research are you thinking?"

"Dosage calculations, symptom progression, timing. It would be critical to know when the death would occur to prepare and alibi, don't you think? The question is who among your suspects would have the skills to use that information, not who in the whole area."

I considered this. "Dr. Sterling. She researches these topics for her literature. Edmund runs a small press—he might have access to reference materials through his publishing connections—something more helpful than Wikipedia or Reddit. And Lily; she's been digging into subjects that help with her switch from romance to mystery author."

"But motivation matters too," Elliot pointed out. "Would someone kill over reputation, or is it about money?"

I thought he was being naive about how important reputation was in some circles. "Edmund's business is in serious trouble. Perhaps the payments have pushed him closer to ruin. Publishing at his level isn't really a high margin business."

Our conversation was interrupted by Hardy and Austin's barking. They rushed toward the bookshop and turned around to run back, like they were saying, hurry up it's important.

We ran after the two corgis. We found Malcolm standing outside Hampton's Books, gesturing animatedly at the front door while Austen and Hardy sat at attention, clearly having appointed themselves official alarm system.

"Oh, Ginny! Thank goodness," Malcolm said, his use of my first name a sign of his agitation. "I locked up to take my dinner break and when I got back..." He pointed at the door. "It's been tampered with, hasn't it?"

The lock showed clear signs of forcing, though someone had tried to make it look less obvious. Elliot called DI Drake who arrived within minutes, followed by PC Trewin and the crime scene photographer.

"Professional job," DI Drake observed, examining the mechanism. "Someone knew what they were doing."

"But they made a mess inside," Malcolm added helpfully. "I peeked through the window—I know better than to enter a crime scene. You can see how much has been disturbed."

DI Drake stepped in after warning us not to follow. I got a glimpse before she shut the door, a hurricane wouldn't have done much more damage. Chairs shoved in corners, books tossed on the floor, the door to the office was open. I saw scattered files, then the door shut, and I was left to worry.

PC Trewin reopened the door after a few minutes and beckoned us inside. "You'll need to work out if anything is missing."

"I'll keep the dogs," Elliot said. "You don't need distractions."

"It will take some time," I said surveying the disaster. "But it does look like the worst is in the office. Whoever did this knows how a bookstore works, I think." I pointed out the broken drawers. "Orders, and publisher correspondence. I have no idea what they would find, but it's definitely about the business not the books themselves."

"We know someone who fits that bill." DI Drake was already on her radio. "Bring in Edmund Fitzmoore for questioning immediately."

"What about this possible gangster?" I asked. "It does feel a lot like someone who's comfortable in the breaking and entering world had a hand in this."

"Gangsters!" Malcolm said. "We have actual gangsters in town?"

DI Drake gave me a look like I'd spilled state secrets. "We don't know for certain. Please don't inflame the situation. We have a perfectly good suspect."

As the police finished processing the crime scene, I stood in my violated but still beloved bookshop, surrounded by neighbors offering practical support. The murder investigation was reaching its climax, my romantic clarity had emerged from crisis, and someone had tried to frighten me into what? Leaving, providing information? Handing over a victim for questioning in a damp basement before being fitted for cement shoes? *Get a grip.*

"It would appear the crime is contained on this floor," DI Drake said. "What's upstairs?"

"Rare books, supplies. Freya's apartment," I said suddenly very grateful she was out of town.

"Let me check," Malcolm said. He hurried up the stairs at a pace I'd never seen before.

We heard his footsteps cross the floor and go up the next flight to Freya's. Then he called down to let us know nothing had been touched.

"So it looks like you're right," DI Drake said. "Something to do with your business not your stock."

13

—————

I didn't feel like shutting the shop and hiding at home. I
suppose I was avoiding Beau, he was there managing
his latest crisis, and I didn't want to get annoyed and
start a conversation we wouldn't have time to finish.

I let Malcolm deal with the stream of villagers looking
for gossip—he enlisted them in the process of cleaning up
—and tackled the office. It was oddly calming to gather all
the papers and folders into one messy pile and start putting
everything in the right place. Austin and Hardy snoozed in
their dog beds, satisfied I didn't need their help for a while.

I had made significant progress, having filled half the
folders with the right papers, when I lifted an invoice to find
an envelop that didn't fit with the rest. Heavy ivory paper,
like a wedding invitation, nothing on the front.

I opened it carefully, expecting perhaps a threatening
note. Instead, I found photocopied documents—bank statements, email printouts, and what appeared to be a detailed
client ledger with initials, amounts, and payment schedules.
None of it pertaining the Hamptons Books. Had this break

in been to plant evidence? Proof of a motive? Not to frame me, surely there were better targets for that.

The top page bore a handwritten note: *Tobias Fletcher's blackmail records. He was targeting dozens of people throughout the literary community. Edmund Fitzmoore was both victim and business partner. The truth is more complicated than murder. A concerned friend*

"Malcolm," I called, my voice sharper than intended. "You need to see this immediately."

Malcolm emerged from the front carrying his ever-present cup of tea, but his expression shifted to alarm when he saw what I held out. "What exactly are we looking at?"

"Evidence of a blackmail operation," I said, scanning the financial records with growing horror. "We knew about some of these, but not all."

Malcolm examined the documents. "These appear to be genuine financial records. Bank routing numbers, transaction dates, even coded references to what he calls consultation services." He paused at the sentence that shocked me. "Edmund Fitzmoore was part of this? Shocking."

Before we could discuss what to do with it, Dot Jenkins popped her head through the doorway.

"Ginny, dear, we need to talk immediately," Dot announced, clutching her gardening gloves and looking thoroughly flustered. "Someone's been stealing from my garden."

"What kind of stealing?" I asked, though given everything we'd learned, I suspected I already knew.

"Foxglove," Dot said grimly. "Several mature plants, dug up root and all. And not by someone who knew what they were doing, or perhaps they knew but didn't care. They left a proper mess." Dot's plantings were less like a cottage garden than a botanical display. She'd notice if someone dared to deadhead her dahlias without permission.

Elspeth stepped in behind Dot. "I saw someone in Dot's garden Tuesday evening, around nine o'clock. Thought it was just Dot doing late evening watering, but when she mentioned it this morning I thought again. The person was too tall to be her. I couldn't get a good look at them, sorry."

"I was in bed by nine-thirty Tuesday," Dot said firmly. "Whoever took my foxglove knew exactly when I'd be asleep and it's not like I have locks on the gate."

Malcolm offered tea and went to put the kettle on while we absorbed this news. "Dot, during our walk through your Victorian garden, did anyone show particular interest in your foxglove plants?"

"That Dr. Sterling asked very detailed questions about poison gardens. Very popular in the Victorian times. I don't have one specifically, but a lot of plants are deadly. I decided not to tempt anyone by labeling a section as killer plants," Dot replied. "That Edmund Fitzmoore was the one who seemed most knowledgeable about the use of poison in literature."

"Did he tell you anything new?" I asked. I didn't want to sound like I was interrogating her on a credible suspect, but I needed to know.

She tipped her head to the side as if thinking. "The book details were interesting. I didn't know that poisoners would soak paper in toxic water."

It was time to bring in the experts. I sent a text to DI Drake that we had information for her and Malcolm returned with Earl Grey tea and biscuits.

It took the police moments to arrive, which made me suspect they were closer than the converted town hall.

"Ginny," DI Drake said after ordering PC Trewin to get

statements from Dot and Elspeth. "We've made some significant discoveries about Fletcher's activities." She paused, noticing the other occupants of the room and the printouts spread across my desk. "It looks like we aren't the only ones."

I handed her the anonymous envelope and its contents. "Someone left these in the mess they made of the files. They show Fletcher wasn't working alone."

Dot drained her tea and said, "we'll let you get on with it. You know where to find us." Elspeth followed her out.

I'd pass on the garden information to DI Drake when we finished with the documents.

She flipped through the papers and then handed them to the PC to be put into evidence. "This changes things," she said when he left. "Mr. Fitzmoore has more motive than any of the others. If some east-end gang is on the hunt, he'd want to cut all ties to the crime."

"What's your news?" I asked.

"We dug deeper into the files. A search warrant was carried out on Fletcher's home. We found many more victims, but not how to break his code."

"How many?" Malcolm asked. "I mean, its' not exactly a big world. Is the entire industry corrupt?"

"I'm sure not all of them," she said. "If it's that big, we might not be able to call it a crime. Defense barristers would claim it's just how business is done."

I thought of the few scandals in the US where that defense had failed. Of course, there could be more where it worked and the results were under a gag order.

"Based on his files, at least forty active cases, with evidence suggesting he'd been building this network for over ten years." DI Drake pulled a file from her satchel. "But here's what's particularly interesting—some of these people weren't just victims."

She handed me a series of business correspondence. I scanned the contents. What had started as blackmail had evolved into something more complex—partnerships, referral agreements, and profit-sharing arrangements. Like this was a legitimate business and a victim could become a partner by referring—ratting on—someone else.

"Fletcher was recruiting some of his victims to become accomplices," I said, hoping I'd misunderstood.

"Exactly. Although no one stopped paying their own blackmail, just seemed to get a discount. And Edmund Fitzmoore appears to have been his primary business partner." DI Drake pulled out a thick folder labeled Fitzmoore Small Press Client Services. "We executed a search warrant on his offices earlier, too."

"Edmund wasn't just being blackmailed," DI Drake continued. "He was running a comprehensive fraud operation, producing fake degrees, forged letters of recommendation, and false professional certifications."

Malcolm examined the photographs with obvious distress. "The scale of this operation..."

"Over three hundred fake credentials produced in the past eighteen months alone," DI Drake said. "PhD certificates from Oxford, Cambridge, Edinburgh. Letters of recommendation from professors who don't exist. Authentication documents for manuscripts that were created last month but altered to look like they came from the Victorian era."

The sophistication was staggering. I studied photographs of Edmund's client database, seeing names, payment records, and detailed notes about each custom credential request. The financial amounts were enormous—individual fake PhDs selling for £5,000 to £15,000, depending on the prestige of the supposed institution. Oxford, Cambridge, Stanford, Yale, Harvard. Every one of the top universities.

"But how did Fletcher figure this operation would work?" I asked.

"We don't know yet," DI Drake said. "All the documents are blank templates, so we still have no names. No one to interview and turn against him—a dead man. He'd identified Edmund as a potential target through small conference attendance records, then systematically investigated his business practices until he uncovered the credential fraud operation. That's the theory right now."

"Then he decided that a partner who paid him was far better than a victim," Malcolm said. "It's like a mystery novel."

"It looks like Fletcher threatened to expose Edmund unless he agreed to partnership terms," DI Drake continued. "This is speculation of course. Until we can get Fitzmoore's confession."

"Does that mean Fitzmoore killed Fletcher to end the partnership? Or to take it over?" I had a hard time understanding the motivation of a man who seemed so meek.

14

The shop bell chimed, and Malcolm went to see to the customer. "Have you arrested him?" I asked.

"Not yet," DI Drake said. "If we do that too soon, it will be hard to have him charged. I don't want to give him warning to get his story in place. This is five percent fact and ninety-five percent speculation. I want to arrest and charge him in one go. Saves us from chasing him down when he runs."

"You have a visitor," Malcolm said as he ushered Edmund Fitzmoore into the office. His usually immaculate appearance was disheveled, his hands shook slightly, and he carried a leather portfolio like it was a dead rodent.

"DI Drake," he said, "I believe it's time we had an honest conversation about my relationship with Tobias Fletcher."

She didn't show any sign that this was old information, simply gestured for him to sit on the remaining vacant chair. Malcolm closed the office door and left us alone. I was happy to be included rather than sent out too.

DI Drake took out her phone and set it on the desk to

record. She gave the time and attendees then started officially. "Mr. Fitzmoore, before you say anything, I should inform you that you're not under arrest, but anything you tell us may be used as evidence."

"I understand," Edmund said. "I want to tell you everything about Fletcher's blackmail operation and my involvement in it. I can't live with the lies any longer."

He opened his portfolio and spread additional documents across our already crowded surface—contracts, financial agreements, and what appeared to be a detailed business plan for expanding the enterprise. I recognized a few of the documents from DI Drake's evidence, but there were many more that we hadn't seen.

"Tobias Fletcher was brilliant at identifying people with questionable credentials," Edmund began. "He'd attend literary conferences, academic symposiums, publishing events, then research anyone who was presenting themselves as experts. Most people were legitimate."

That was a relief. I'd started to think Beau and I were the only honest people in the industry. "And when they weren't?" I asked. "Like Dr. Sterling?"

"Exactly. Tobias could spot inconsistencies in people's academic references that most wouldn't notice. Well, I suppose it's more accurate to say no one else would care. Then he'd verify his suspicions through direct contact with universities and employers." Edmund's voice carried a mixture of admiration and revulsion. "Once he confirmed someone had false credentials, he'd approach them with evidence and demands for payment."

"But you became his business partner," DI Drake observed.

"Yes. Fletcher realized that blackmailing people with fake credentials was less profitable than using them to find more victims." Edmund met our shocked expressions with resigned honesty. "He proposed a partnership—anyone who brought in new victims would get a discount of ten percent."

The business model was as logical as it was criminal. Fletcher's research skills combined with Edmund's technical capabilities had created a comprehensive credential fraud enterprise serving desperate academics, struggling writers, and ambitious professionals throughout the literary community.

"What went wrong?" I asked.

"Tobias became greedy. He wanted to start providing fakes. He called it vertical integration. Pay for the fake documents, be blackmailed for using the documents, and be rewarded for bringing others into the network." Edmund's hands trembled as he reached for his portfolio. "It was getting too big. The chance we would run into someone who'd rather go to the police was getting too high."

"It's a wonder he wasn't reported before this," DI Drake said grimly.

"He was going to destroy hundreds of people's lives just to increase profit margins." Edmund's voice cracked. "I couldn't deal with the stress."

"So you killed him," I said. I was tired of his waffling.

"No! I'm not a killer. My plan was to come clean, face the consequences. I told him that. It felt fair to give him a chance to join me, but..."

"But he wasn't interested," DI Drake said.

"No, and then he was dead. I thought that meant it was over, but I can't sleep, I keep thinking it's my fault for going along with it. I feel like an idiot, I paid him thousands of pounds even though we were partners, he never gave me back the evidence."

DI Drake stood and went through the process of

arresting Edmund for the crimes he'd actually committed, but I wasn't convince she believed he was innocent of murder.

15

I found the threatening note when I arrived at Hampton's Books that morning, slipped under the front door like a malevolent calling card. The paper was ordinary—the kind you could buy at any village shop—but the message was clear.

Stop interfering, or there will be consequences for the entire village. Some accidents can't be prevented.

"Well," I said to Austen and Hardy, who were sniffing the note with obvious disapproval, "that's not exactly the warm morning greeting I was hoping for."

Captain appeared from upstairs, took one look at the paper in my hands, and promptly meowed his disapproval. For a cat who wandered in and out of my life, he was quite protective.

"Quite right, Captain," I murmured, though my hands were shaking as I photographed the note so I'd have a copy when I handed it over to DI Drake. "Anonymous threats are definitely beneath our dignity."

I knew the case was still active. Unlike DI Drake, I

believed Edmund. Why would he have admitted everything else and not the murder?

When I got home last night, I wanted to talk to Beau about the events, but he was tied up on a call so I didn't interrupt him. Choosing instead to mull everything over myself. Of course that didn't lead to any conclusions about the real killer.

The shop felt different this morning—too quiet, too watchful. Even the familiar scent of old books and lavender polish couldn't dispel the sense that someone had violated our peaceful sanctuary. I found myself checking shadows and listening for footsteps that weren't there.

The kettle was just beginning to whistle in the back room when Elspeth tapped gently at the door, holding up a plate of fresh scones. I let her in, grateful for the company.

"Saw your lights on early, dear," she said, bustling inside. "Thought you might need proper breakfast after last night's excitement."

"Last night's excitement?" Had the rumor mill already spread the news?

"The prowler, dear. Tried your back door around five this morning—bold as brass, they were. I was starting the baking when I saw it." She set the scones on the counter and patted my arm sympathetically. "Whoever it was scattered quick enough when they heard me shouting."

That must be who delivered the note. At least the new locks had held, I wouldn't need to install alarms and iron bars. "Did you see who it was?"

"Too dark, and they were wearing one of those hooded things. But they knew what they were about—no fumbling or amateur hour. Went straight for the lock like they had tools." Her eyes sparkled with satisfaction at being the first to inform me. "Probably after the till, that thug who came down from London I expect. I didn't call your DI because she doesn't have time for petty crimes. She needs to solve the murder."

I didn't agree but then it was before I got the threat, so maybe I would have done the same. "I'm sure that person has left," I said. "Gone back to London. Not much here to attract real criminals."

"I know what you mean," Elspeth said. "But don't you dismiss murder as nothing."

Malcolm arrived on time, carrying his umbrella despite the clear morning and wearing an expression that suggested he'd already heard village gossip about our nocturnal visitor. I wondered if there was some app I needed to download to stay current.

"Miss Hampton," he said, hanging his umbrella on its designated hook with particular care, "I trust you suffered no ill effects from last night's disturbance?"

"Other than feeling like I'm living in one of our mystery novels? I'm fine." Did I imagine the confession? Or was the village more interested in current gossip than a days old crime?

Before I could tell Malcolm about the threat, I noticed someone approaching the shop. Oliver. Finally back, although I didn't think anyone would be interested in a literary walk today.

The shop bell chimed as he entered, but instead of his usual calculating smile, he looked genuinely unsettled.

"Ginny, thank God you're all right. I heard about the break-in attempt." He paused as if waiting for me to comment. "Though it seems you're well looked after."

"News travels fast in the village," I observed, glad I kept the note to myself for now. A call to DI Drake could wait until I had some peace.

"Faster when it involves criminal activity at beloved local institutions." Oliver announced. "Which is why I need to tell you something. About the paper."

"Paper? What paper?"

"From the crime scene," Oliver said, his antiques dealer's instincts apparently overriding any concerns about sharing police information with the village gossip network. "The investigators asked me to identify it yesterday. As soon as I got home, I didn't even have time to unpack."

Malcolm set down the teapot. "And you were able to help them?"

"Oh you don't know the half of it." Oliver paused again for effect. "Handmade reproduction parchment worth a few pounds. They altered it, can you believe the audacity? Selling it as an original. I can't believe he's tarnished my reputation. I've been selling similar items to Edmund Fitz-moore for months."

"Did you tell DI Drake that?" I reached for my phone to text her but waited for his answer.

"Yes." Oliver snapped. "And I've been an absolute fool. I would prefer to keep it private, but I assume I'll be the object of derision soon enough."

Malcolm poured Oliver a cup of tea. "A lot happened while you were gone."

"Yes, another murder." He took a sip and nodded his approval. "I know you are poking your nose in since our tour has become a spectacular failure. I might as well tell you everything. Six months ago, Edmund started placing orders for specialty papers. Claimed he needed them for authentication work—testing historical manuscripts, creating comparison samples for fraud detection." Oliver took another sip as if to calm himself. "But the forensics team showed me exactly which paper was found at the crime scene. It wasn't just any historical parchment—it was premium reproduction vellum, the kind that can be used for plays, or television, or movies, or for creating convincing fake academic documents."

"Forged certifications," I said. "Or old manuscripts that need to be authenticated?"

Oliver waved he free hand around to punctuate his disgust at the actions of his customers. "Not so much degrees, letters of recommendation, those are modern paper. But rare manuscripts. As a document from the same time period, yes. Often that's used to prove the age of a document, mentioned in someone's diary for example. Anything someone might need to establish false credentials in the literary world." He pulled a small notebook from his jacket pocket. "I've been going through my records since yesterday. Edmund's purchases were escalating."

He opened the notebook, revealing detailed entries in his meticulous handwriting. "February: basic parchment samples and aging inks. March: specialized letterheads matching Oxford and Cambridge designs. April: sealing wax and authentication stamps."

Malcolm's eyebrows went up. "That's a complete forger's toolkit for academic credentials."

"It gets worse." Oliver turned several pages. "May: bulk orders of premium vellum specifically aged to diffcrent periods. June: he heard I found an antique press. Not a very valuable one, but useful in what we now know about his crimes."

It felt like we knew the extent of the criminal enterprise and then more information rose to the surface. "Multiple clients?"

"At least six separate document sets, based on the quantities. And he was willing to pay triple my usual rates for immediate delivery." Oliver's voice cracked. "I thought he was just being thorough about authentication testing, but now..."

"Now it looks like he was preparing to forge credentials for everyone Tobias might investigate," I finished.

Malcolm had been studying Oliver's notebook. "The timeline is particularly damning. I'll need to check but it looks like Edmund's orders increased dramatically after each literary conference or academic gathering. Times when he would have been making new contacts who might need... credential enhancement."

"There's more," Oliver said grimly. "Yesterday, after Edmund came forward with his blackmail confession—yes, we all heard about it—I received a rather frantic phone call. He wanted to know if I'd kept detailed records of our transactions, whether the police had been in touch, and—most tellingly—whether the paper could be traced to specific batches."

"What did you tell him?"

"The truth. That I maintain meticulous records for insurance purposes, and that each batch of specialty parchment has unique watermarks and composition markers." Oliver's expression suggested he now understood the significance of Edmund's reaction. "He went very quiet, then asked if I'd be willing to misplace certain invoices for a substantial fee."

The shop fell silent except for the ticking of the old mantle clock. Captain, sensing the gravity of the conversation, padded over to Oliver's chair and began his therapeutic purring routine.

"He tried to bribe you to destroy evidence?" Malcolm asked.

"And when I refused, he became quite agitated. Started

talking about how the records would incriminate him in crimes he didn't commit. A killer getting away with it because the police would stop looking."

"It seems we have the real reason he chose to confess," Malcolm said. "I assume he thought his punishment would be less severe if he turned himself in."

"Exactly," Oliver said. "We should talk to your DI together, Ginny. Make sure she doesn't get side tracked."

16

Before any of us could fully process Oliver's revelation, DI Drake entered the bookshop with PC Trewin in tow, both looking official and carrying evidence bags.

"Miss Hampton," DI Drake said, glancing around at our assembled group. "I see the village communication network is operating efficiently. Good—we need to discuss what we found during our examination of last night's break-in."

"Why didn't you call me when someone tried to get in?" I asked.

"They didn't get in," DI Drake said. "I don't need you sleep deprived. I have that in spades. I need you alert."

That seemed a little self-serving, but I didn't argue. She didn't know about the threat.

PC Trewin set an evidence bag on the counter, revealing a leather folder with what I guess were lock-picking tools. "Whoever attempted entry was no amateur. These were left behind when Mrs. Willoughby's shouting startled them into fleeing."

Elspeth hadn't needed to call the police, someone did it for her.

"These tools tell us something important about who we're dealing with." DI Drake accepted Malcolm's offer of tea. "The attempt was methodical and targeted. They may have been the same people who broke in earlier. We have no evidence that the second attempt was successful, but did anything seem out of place this morning?"

Time to come clean. "There was a threatening note inside. I think it was pushed under the door."

"What?" Oliver sat up and glared at me. "Why didn't you say something?"

"Ms. Hampton," Malcolm said with a little more decorum but a lot more implied criticism. "You should have called DI Drake immediately. What would Dr. Harrington think? Or your American friend? How are we to keep you safe?"

I almost snapped at them that I could take care of myself, but managed to hold the words back. "I was going to call, but Oliver came in and I got distracted. I was in no immediate danger."

I handed the envelope with the note inside to DI Drake. She read it and gave it to PC Trewin to put in an evidence bag. "This sounds more like our London gangster than Mr. Fitzmoore. I'll have it tested for fingerprints. We'll arrange for your protection, Ginny. It seems your instinct was right. We still have a killer on the loose."

"Why would I be threatened?" I asked. "I'm not part of this scheme. Just a business woman trying to draw tourists to our village."

"The killer might not know that," Oliver said. "They may think you're the mastermind. You brought people together, all of whom are involved in one way or another."

"Or they think that Miss Hampton had obtained copies of those files," PC Trewin added, consulting his notebook.

"We've had no luck identifying our visiting gangster," DI Drake said. "Mrs. Willoughby didn't get a close enough look. Probably for the best." DI Drake produced another evidence bag containing a small piece of paper. "We found this near the dropped lock-picks. It's a fragment of the same specialty parchment Mr. Blackthorn has been selling."

The implications hit the room like a physical blow. Oliver went pale. "I am not a criminal, I a victim in this."

"Yes, we know," DI Trewin said. "We think someone was trying to take over the operation. Problem with being successful as a criminal. There's always someone meaner who wants a cut or to shut you down."

I was beginning to accept that I needed protection. "I don't understand why a professional would threaten the entire village. Surely that just draws more attention to his criminal activities?"

DI Drake exchanged glances with PC Trewin. "We aren't sure how much Edmund knows about this, but it seems Mr. Fletcher was dipping his toes into the world of money laundering."

"Money laundering?" Malcolm asked. "But that's international. I was reading an article just last week about it."

"And it would draw more than a London crime family." DI Drake stood. "This is all speculation. I don't want the village alarmed. Just careful. And to report anything suspicious to me immediately."

"I'll get on it right away," Elspeth said. She'd been quietly sitting in the corner unnoticed during the whole conversation. "Don't you worry, Ginny. We'll keep everyone safe."

As if summoned by our discussion of security arrangements, Elliot opened the door and joined us.

"Dr. Harrington," Elspeth said. "Perfect timing. We were just discussing protective measures for Ginny."

"Good to hear. I'm ready to step in with my presence, or perhaps a large dog to supplement your corgis," he said, then addressed DI Drake directly and held out a sheet of dirty paper. "I have some information for you."

She took the document he handed her. "Where did you find this?"

"In the grounds keeper's cottage, the abandoned one, past the church. The vicar called because she'd heard barking inside. Thought an animal was in distress. Not only was she right, but someone was squatting there in the last couple of days. Gone now, but a collie was trapped inside."

"Oh dear," Elspeth said. "John Markham was telling me his Pepper was missing."

"I returned Pepper before coming here," Elliot said. "She's fine, just hungry and thirsty. But she was guarding that."

"Good dog," PC Trewin said. Both Hardy and Austin perked up, prepared to take any credit whether they earned it or not. "Seems odd that the squatter didn't just move her to take the papers."

"We can always ask when you catch him," Elliot said. "Not simply a squatter. Someone who means harm."

"And perhaps proof that Edmund was telling the truth." DI Drake stood and infuriatingly didn't share the contents of the document. Her ability to change her mind so quickly about the identity of the killer might be open-mindedness, or uncertainty. I hoped for the first.

"Mr. Blackthorn, you're coming to the town hall now for that statement—and protective custody if necessary. Miss

Hampton, you're not to be alone under any circumstances until we locate Edmund."

"What about the shop?" I asked. "I can't just close Hampton's Books because some criminal made threats."

"You're not closing," Elspeth announced. "We're implementing community protection measures. Rotating volunteer presence. We'll coordinate with whatever the police have in mind. Everyone will keep eyes open for anything unusual. We are not letting anyone come in and destroy our village."

It seemed I had no say in the matter. As we began organizing what was essentially a village-wide protection network, I watched Elliot. He was quietly efficient in the way he coordinated with PC Trewin to keep everyone safe. Nothing about him said he had other, more important things to do.

There was something deeply reassuring about his presence that went beyond the current crisis. Not dramatic romantic gesture or possessive protection, just steady reliability and genuine care that made even the threat of a desperate criminal feel manageable.

After DI Drake and Oliver departed, the shop gradually settled into its routine—heightened awareness, yes, but still a normal enough day. Neighbors and friends dropped in during the day, browsing or sitting with a book in the reading space. People I hadn't met yet, including the owner of a very protective collie.

"You know," I said to Captain, who had appointed himself my permanent lap guardian, "when I inherited this bookshop, I thought the biggest challenges would be inventory management and customer service."

17

The afternoon light filtering through Hampton's Books felt different today—heavier somehow, as if the very air carried the weight of secrets about to be revealed. Dr. Vivienne Sterling sat in the wingback chair Malcolm had offered, her hands trembling as she accepted a cup of tea from his emergency service set.

"I've been living a lie for seven years," she said, her voice barely above a whisper. "And now I think that lie might get me hanged for murder."

"The death penalty isn't an option any longer." Malcolm settled into his chair with his own cup, his expression professionally neutral but kind. "Perhaps you should start from the beginning, Dr. Sterling."

"That's just it—I'm not Dr. Sterling. Not really." She took a shaky breath. "My PhD isn't from Oxford. It's from Ashford International University, a diploma mill that operates entirely through correspondence. I paid five thousand pounds for a complete academic identity—transcripts, thesis documentation, even a fake thesis adviser who would vouch for my work if anyone called."

The confession hung in the cozy atmosphere of the bookshop like morning fog. No shocked gasps came from our assembled group, simply silence. Lily, Malcolm, and Freya, who had returned only an hour ago—just long enough to get the overview of our case, waited for her to continue.

"Why?" I asked gently.

"Because without credentials, you're nobody in the literary world." Dr. Sterling's voice grew stronger, fueled by years of suppressed frustration. "I'd been working as a freelance researcher for various tour companies, scraping by on local guide wages. The pay difference between knowledgeable amateur and Oxford-educated expert was the difference between poverty and a decent living. No one cares about whether you have the knowledge, just what letters exist after your name."

She set down her teacup and opened her handbag, pulling out a sheaf of paper. "Tobias Fletcher discovered all of this. Tuesday evening, he cornered me in the B&B parlor with a complete dossier on my fabricated background."

The folder she spread on the coffee table contained photocopies of correspondence with Ashford International, bank records showing her payment, and what appeared to be detailed research into Oxford's actual doctoral records.

"He was thorough," Malcolm observed, examining the documents. He made no reference to our prior knowledge of the crimes.

"Terrifyingly thorough. He'd contacted Oxford directly, confirmed that no Vivienne Sterling had ever studied there, and even tracked down the real thesis adviser I'd claimed to work with." Dr. Sterling's laugh held no humor. "The poor man had never heard of me, naturally."

Freya looked up from her notebook where she'd been

documenting the conversation. "How long has Tobias been investigating you?"

"At least six months, based on the dates in his correspondence. He'd been systematically researching everyone involved in literary tourism and authentication in Devon—tour guides, small press publishers, freelance researchers. Looking for vulnerabilities he could exploit."

"What did he want?" Freya asked with an edge to her voice. She'd worked hard for her PhD and carried some debt that would follow her for years. It must rankle hearing that Dr., no, Ms. Sterling had taken a shortcut.

"Initially, he claimed he was writing a hard hitting article about academic fraud in the tourism industry. Said he wanted to interview me about the pressures that lead qualified people to fabricate credentials." Ms. Sterling's voice hardened. "But by Wednesday morning, his demands had evolved considerably."

She pulled out another set of documents—email printouts and handwritten notes. "He wanted me to provide academic endorsement for his manuscript. Dr. Vivienne Sterling of Oxford recommending his work would carry significant weight with publishers, he said."

"How awful. Condemning you and using you at the same time," Lily said with an air of empathy.

Ms. Sterling blotted her eyes with a tissue she pulled from her pocket. "I fear the actual blackmail wouldn't be too far away. He understood exactly how academic careers function—one whisper about fraudulent credentials would destroy not just my current work, but any possibility of legitimate employment anywhere in the literary world. Even my genuine expertise would be dismissed as worthless once the fraud was exposed."

Captain jumped onto Dr. Sterling's lap, beginning his

therapeutic purring and kneading routine while she stroked his fur with automatic motions.

"The cruel irony," she continued, "is that my knowledge of Victorian literature is entirely authentic. I've spent fifteen years in intensive self-study, reading every major work, following current scholarship, auditing lectures whenever possible. I could discuss Gaskell's industrial novels or the influence of Gothic elements on sensational fiction with complete authority. But none of that matters without the proper paperwork."

"Which brings us to the obvious question," I said. "Did you kill Tobias Fletcher?"

"No." The answer came without hesitation. "Though I understand why I'm your primary suspect. Someone with botanical knowledge, being blackmailed by the victim, desperate enough to commit fraud. It's a compelling case. I hear they've arrested Fitzmoore, but not for murder."

"You don't know his role in the scheme?" I asked curious to see if she was hiding something.

"He was involved?" Ms. Sterling asked. "I assumed... well, that he was a victim."

I noticed Lily react as well, but she didn't speak.

I studied the documents spread before us. Was there something in them to solve the murder? Had we missed a pattern? A thought occurred to me. "Dr. Sterling, who else knew about your credential fraud before Tobias exposed it?"

"No one. I've been extraordinarily careful—"

"But Tobias found you out," Freya said. "Those of us who work for our Doctorate don't see your pretense as an option. So he could have told anyone, and if Fitzmoore was working with him, then that's another way the information could have leaked."

Freya was able to call herself doctor now but chose not

to. I knew it wasn't just about the work involved. She'd made sacrifices to become legitimate. And she worked in my bookstore rather than using her hard won doctorate.

Ms. Sterling went very still. "I didn't tell anyone. Fletcher wouldn't have, don't you think? He wouldn't want the competition."

"Someone knows. If none of you killed him, he's still dead," I said. "We've had evidence that someone from London came down to ask about him. I find it hard to believe any of the London gangs would have waited until he left the city to kill him."

The front door opened, and Edmund Fitzmoore entered. He glanced around and stopped when he saw us. Saying he looked nervous would be like saying the ocean was big. I almost expected him to faint.

"Am I interrupting something?" he asked, taking in our assembled group, and the documents spread across the coffee table. "Or are you discussing my shortfalls?"

"How are you free?" Lily asked. "You were partners with that horrible man."

"My solicitor arranged for me to be release on the promise I would turn up for my court date." He lifted his trouser leg. "Tracker to keep me close. Please, believe me when I say I didn't kill him. My crimes are what they call white collar. No violence, no need to keep me in custody."

Before anyone could utter another word, Captain suddenly hissed and bolted toward the back of the shop, his fur standing on end. Both dogs began growling low in their throats, their attention fixed on something beyond our view.

"Someone's in the back room," I whispered.

Malcolm moved with surprising stealth toward the back of the shop, while I motioned for everyone else to stay quiet. But before we could investigate further, we heard the distinct sound of the back door slamming closed.

Someone had been listening to our entire conversation. Someone who now knew exactly how much we'd discovered about the blackmail scheme.

Someone who might be desperate enough to ensure we never shared that knowledge with DI Drake.

Malcolm returned from the back of the shop, his expression grim. "Whoever it was has gone."

"How long were they listening?" Ms. Sterling asked, her voice tight with fear.

"Long enough to hear everything we know," I said. "Long enough to know we've figured out that someone used your credential fraud to make you look guilty."

When we returned to the seating area, Lily was gone.

I sent a text to DI Drake. She ordered us to stay in place and she would join us when the search was organized. "Don't be surprised if a PC comes to check the scene."

"We need to think about this calmly," Malcolm said, resuming his seat and reaching to test the heat of the teapot. "Who else was staying at the B&B with access to Tobias's research?"

"Lily, she was here a minute ago, and Edmund," I said. "There were no other guests, although two rooms were vacant."

"Who else knew about the literary tour participants in advance?" Freya asked

"Mrs. Pengelly, obviously. The tour organizer at the tourist board. Anyone involved in organizing the weekend," I replied.

"Who else has botanical knowledge sufficient to prepare foxglove poison properly?" Malcolm continued.

We all looked at each other, the obvious suspects already

revealed. But something nagged at me—a detail I couldn't quite place.

"Ms. Sterling," I said, as I let the thought percolate, "when you met with tour participants on Tuesday evening, did anyone ask specifically about your botanical expertise?"

She thought for a moment. "Several people commented on my knowledge during the garden portion of the tour. Lily was particularly interested in the poisonous plants section. She said she was researching Victorian murder methods for her novel."

"Lily," Freya repeated, her pen hovering over her notebook.

"She's been taking detailed notes throughout the weekend," I realized. "Notes about everyone and everything."

"Including all our discussions about people's vulnerabilities," Malcolm added. "Professional jealousies, financial pressures, personal secrets."

The shop bell chimed again. But instead of Lily, a breathless PC Trewin entered, clearly bearing urgent news.

"DI Drake told me to come," he said, "we found something in Miss Ashworth's room at the B&B. A complete dossier on Tobias Fletcher's blackmail operation, including financial projections and victim profiles."

"She was sitting here talking to us only moments ago," Ms. Sterling said. "Where is she?"

"Not in her room." PC Trewin spoke into the radio. "Not here either."

Right after the discovery of our eavesdropper. "She can't be far," I said. "Are her things still in her room?"

"Yes, unless she's abandoning her belongings, she won't have left the village." PC Trewin listened to something on the radio and nodded toward the back room. "I'll be looking for evidence of your most recent visitor, or leads in the back. I'll let you know when I'm done."

When we were alone, I returned to our discussion. "She used your secret, Vivienne to deflect suspicion," I said, understanding flooding through me. "She knew about the credential fraud, the botanical knowledge, the blackmail pressure. You were the perfect scapegoat."

"But why kill Tobias?" Edmund asked. "What was her motive? She wasn't part of the scheme. As far as I know."

18

PC was posted at our back door and I was feeling quite safe. Malcolm had left for the day and Freya had gone up to her apartment above the store. She promised to return to help me lock up after she'd unpacked and cleaned up. I could have let her take care of everything, but I was looking forward to a chat about her trip. And I couldn't quite get comfortable leaving her here alone after two incidents. It wouldn't be the first time for the three of us to share my cottage.

Five minutes to go, and Lily Ashford hurried inside. She looked disheveled as if she'd been running since she left us.

"Please let me explain before you call DI Drake," she said, settling into the armchair out of sight of anyone looking in the window.

Austin and Hardy gave me no hint that she was a danger, and Captain was nowhere to be seen, so I picked up my phone and joined her. "I can't give you much time," I said. "The whole force is out looking for you."

I poured tea from the pot I'd prepared—Malcolm's influence had made tea, a sacred ritual that usually relaxed people. I still preferred coffee, but I was getting used to the alternative.

"Since everyone is looking for you, how did you get here?"

She smiled. "All those times I was late because I go lost," she said putting air quotes around the last word. "I was scouting the village. Found a few back ways to everywhere."

I certainly hoped her explanation would tell me why she'd felt the need to lie. "Why did you run away?" I asked.

A rueful smile crossed her face. "I had to check in with someone. When we heard the person in the back, I didn't know if I should come clean, or continue with my cover."

"Your cover?" Was she a spy? The money laundering could bring forth a lot of international attention, I suppose.

"Yes, I've been acting a role," she admitted quietly. "My name is Lily Ashworth, and I do write romances, but my day job is as an investigative journalist. I write for *Publishing Weekly* under several pen names, but my specialty is exposing fraud within supposedly trusted institutions and industries. There is a lot of it in various forms."

The admission hung between us while I processed this revelation. It explained so much—her familiarity with publishing industry terminology, her sharp questions about credentials, the way she'd watched Edmund during his authentication discussions with the focus of someone building a case. And why DI Drake didn't know she was undercover.

"You've been exposing the scheme?"

"For the past six months, investigating a network that stretches across the UK academic and literary communities. But this weekend..." She paused, stroking Austen's soft ears. "I realized I'd found something much larger than expected. Tobias wasn't just running a simple blackmail operation—

he was at the center of a systematic fraud network. But you know all that now."

I leaned forward, my tea forgotten. "Is there more? We need to bring in DI Drake. You may have something that will point to the murderer."

Lily pulled out a notebook from her bag. The same one I'd seen her writing in throughout the tour, though now I understood it contained evidence rather than story ideas. "I'm not sure I have more than you know already. The connection to the London gangs is new to me. I might be able to find out who that was."

I felt a chill run through me. "That will be dangerous. The police will handle it." I pulled out my phone, but she asked for a few more minutes.

"I learned at the same time you did that Edmund was part of the whole thing. Embarrassing really, I should have seen it right away."

"I wouldn't have guessed if he didn't admit it," I said. "Do you have something to add. If he should be held in custody, we should pass it along."

"I don't have proof." She clutched the notebook to her as if I was about to rip it away. "I could lose my job if I give out information that other publications get to first."

"And someone else could die if you don't," I said, having little patience with the attitude. "You said you had to check with someone before speaking, who? And what did they say?"

"My editor. He said it was up to me."

"Then tell us," I said. "How will you feel if someone is hurt because you kept silent?"

"Awful, of course," she said. "It's hard to change a lifetime of habit. Sharing information is something I've always resisted."

Elliot joined us before I could press Lily, or call DI Drake.

"I came to see if you would like to join me for dinner," he said. "If your guest is still sorting out his work problems."

I had no intention of telling Elliot that Beau was in fact ignoring me for this emergency. "I would love to, but I may be with DI Drake for a while."

"Happy to wait," he said. "Can I help in any way?"

It would be nice to have an ally. Perhaps he could call for official help while I kept Lily talking.

"Join us, you might have some insight," I said, pointing him to a vacant chair. "Lily was about to explain why she thinks her professional secrecy is a good reason to withhold information from the police in a murder case."

She flinched at my words, but I didn't feel remorse.

"I'll tell you," she said. "Then you can decide what we pass on. I don't expect to see my article in the local paper. I do expect you to be as careful with my work as I am."

"I won't tell the press," I said. "I'm sure DI Drake will want to keep what you've learned quiet."

Before she could speak, we were joined by DI Drake herself. I was starting to wonder if Hampton Books was the village hub.

"Ginny, there's been a development." She noticed Lily and Elliot and "We've spent a lot of resources looking for you, Ms. Ashworth."

"Am I suspect?" Lily's uncertainty was gone. "I didn't do anything illegal."

I suppose being undercover required her to be a good actor. I wondered if she'd been putting on the frightened act for me, or was this defiant woman the act? Or were they both not the real Lily Ashworth?

"What kind of development?" I asked, hoping to keep us on track.

"A communication. From Mr. Fitzmoore to an associate in London. He's asked for help in dealing with a problem. A nosy bookshop owner and a posse of idiots who might stumble onto the truth."

"Who is the associate?" Elliot asked, immediately moving closer to my chair. "What's being done about the threat? Where are the other participants?"

"We've increased surveillance on the shop and Ms. Hampton's cottage. I have a PC with Ms. Pengelly, and I see Ms. Ashford is here."

"This associate," I said. "Do we know who?"

"Are you sure it came from Edmund?" Lily asked at the same time. "I've been watching him for months. He's not the kind of man to call a hit. Or know who to contact if he got that desperate."

I turned to Lily, startled. "Good point. I think it's time you told DI Drake everything."

A slight flush crossed her cheeks. "I don't have any information on hit men."

"What everything?" DI Drake asked. "Where did you go earlier?"

Lily told DI Drake what she'd already shared with me. I knew she was holding back whatever had been interrupted, but it wasn't my place to press.

"And you called your editor?" DI Drake's tone was harsh.

"Yes, I'm a reporter, that's what we do," Lily snapped. "Am I getting protection? I am part of the idiot posse after all."

"If Fitzmoore is planning something dramatic, he may choose a location with symbolic significance," Elliot said. "The bookshop, obviously. Any of your tour stops."

"All under surveillance," DI Drake confirmed. "But your local knowledge is valuable. Any other locations he might find significant?"

As they discussed possible scenarios and security measures, I found myself thinking about the scope of what we'd uncovered. Not just a simple murder case, but a network of fraud that had affected dozens of lives across the country, including London gangsters and possibly international money laundering.

"How is the investigation going," I asked. From the discussion, the police had made progress, and I had no idea what was going on.

"We've asked for help in contacting the victims of the blackmail," DI Drake said. "Interviewing them will turn up some new details, always does. Here, we're still looking for whoever was in the back room today, and who broke in if they aren't the same person. It won't be long until we solve this, Ginny."

The weight of this settled over all of us. Outside the window, Mrs. Patterson walked by with her ancient corgi, stopping to peer through the glass with obvious curiosity about our crowded gathering. I suppose she could be on a patrol shift, village protection teams at work. I gave her a reassuring wave, though I felt anything but reassured.

DI Drake stood to leave, gathering her materials. "We're hoping for resolution within the next twenty-four hours. We haven't taken Fitzmoore into custody because we want him to make his next move. Either he'll attempt to flee—in which case we'll arrest him. Or his contact will respond. Or we'll prove he didn't send it. Either way, we're prepared."

After the officers left, we sat in contemplative silence, each processing the weight of recent revelations. Hardy had claimed a sunny spot near the window, while Austen maintained her vigil by my feet.

A few hours later, Beau sent me a text asking why there was a cop outside the cottage. I updated him and asked if his situation back home had cleared.

His reply was amusing, but it confirmed his job was continuing to take up all the time he'd planned to spend with me.

I didn't share any of this with the people around me. Freya had joined us, Malcolm had returned, and we were a worried but safe group.

Lily spent a lot of time texting with her editor, I hoped she was making arrangements to share her knowledge. Or perhaps I was wrong, and she was identifying the gang member who'd disturbed us.

Just as I was wondering how to feed the troops, Ms. Sterling entered. I did have trouble not thinking of her as doctor, but I made the effort.

"I've brought provisions," she announced, setting the basket on the counter. "Homemade soup, fresh bread, and beer. Mrs. Pengelly arranged everything."

I regretted agreeing to stay in the store. We could be out there solving the case. But I could only speak for me, and despite my irritation at being sidelined, I wasn't going to search for a killer by myself. And I would not put any of the people here, in jeopardy.

Malcolm rose to help her unpack the basket. "Thank you, I was beginning to wonder what we'd do for food."

"You know," she said, beginning to arrange items on the counter, "I wanted you to know how grateful I am that this situation has forced me to be open. For the first time in years, I don't feel like I'm living a lie."

As evening approached, the shop filled with the

comfortable atmosphere of friends gathering during uncertain times. We shared food and beer, discussed the implications of the fraud network's exposure, and speculated on the gang connection. Lily didn't give us any more information, but Freya had been researching London crime families. She didn't have a clue as to which one was trying to take over the blackmail, but her stories helped pass the time.

"At least some good will come of this," Lily said, reviewing her notes. "Exposing this network will help protect future victims and might encourage other fraud operations to shut down voluntarily."

"Perhaps academic institutions will find a way to accredit people who haven't met all their regulations, like honorary doctorates," Malcolm said.

"Those don't mean much," Freya said.

Whatever Edmund was planning, or being framed for, whatever final confrontation awaited, I was surrounded by people who'd chosen to stand with me. The web of deception that had brought murder to our village was finally being untangled, revealing not just criminal fraud but systemic problems that drove good people to desperate measures.

I settled back in my chair, watching the familiar street outside begin its transition to night, and realized that despite everything—the murder, the threats, the revelations about nationwide fraud—I'd never felt more at home than I did right now, surrounded by friends who'd become family, in a bookshop that had become the center of something much larger than I'd ever imagined.

The final confrontation was coming, but I wouldn't face it alone.

19

The next morning after spending the night with Beau holed up in the guest room, Elliot on the couch and a PC at the front door for protections, we headed to the teashop. Well, the PC and I went there. Elliot had veterinary appointments, Beau his crises, and all I had was a bookshop and a mystery.

Lily was sitting with Ms. Sterling at a table for four. She waved me over. "This feels rather like hiding," she admitted, glancing toward the street. "Though I suppose if someone's planning murder, a public tea shop isn't the worst place to be."

Elspeth arrived with fresh tea, moving with the brisk determination to keep us both safe and fed. "No one's murdering anyone in my establishment. Bad for business, and my insurance doesn't cover homicide cleanup."

Captain had claimed the windowsill, orange fur gleaming in the sunlight as he watched both our table and the street beyond. His presence wasn't accidental—the ginger tom had insisted on accompanying us and brooked no argument. Well, he was a cat after all.

"Edmund's been staying in his room," Elspeth reported, settling beside us with her own cup. "Mrs. Pengelly says he's barely slept, keeps peering through his curtains every few minutes. Expecting trouble, she thinks."

She seemed to think this was his own doing, and I didn't care to argue with her. That didn't mean I could ignore how he'd be tightly strung. Either he was plotting a way to escape his watchers before his assassin arrived, or worried that someone was setting him up for even more trouble than he was already in.

"Can't blame him." Lily pulled out her notebook. "Your DI told him what they found. He denied making the call, or text. I wish she'd told us the details. The meta data, any names, a time even would help."

Captain stretched as only cats can. A long downward dog move, although I should say downward cat, ending in a wide yawn showing sharp teeth.

Through the glass, I could see Freya approaching with her usual chaotic energy, hair blowing around, laptop bag bouncing against her hip and cardigan falling off one shoulder.

"Reinforcements," Elspeth observed approvingly. "That girl is sharp as razor blades."

When Freya burst through the door, her excitement was barely contained. "I've been in the university databases since dawn. I may have found a link," she announced without preamble.

"Our friend Fletcher wasn't just waiting for people to make mistakes he could exploit. He manufactured evidence."

Lily sat bolt upright. "What? How could he manipulate people who hadn't done anything wrong? How did I miss that?"

"You don't have the same access as I do, or the knowledge to interpret the information. It's easy now to fake anything. I think that's where he got professionals involved." Freya opened her laptop and waited for something load.

"Freya, have you told the police what you found?" Ms. Sterling asked. "If someone knows what you have, they might..."

"Don't worry," Freya said. "I passed everything on before I came. I know my limitations. I can't hack in without leaving a trace. Oh, let's be honest, I can't hack at all. Everything I worked on came from access I had or with DI Drake's approval. I just found the connections."

"So who is this gangster?" I asked, taking her assurance at face value.

"I'll get to that." She turned the screen so we could all see and pointed to a highlighted bank statement. "Edmund Fitzmoore's small press. Regular monthly payments from dozens of people, always for amounts that don't correspond to any legitimate publishing services."

"But how did you connect this to a crime family?" Lily asked.

"Well, as it turns out, I was given access to some of the special crimes unit information." She beamed. "They must trust me. Or perhaps it was a mistake."

"Right. This calls for something stronger than Earl Grey," Elspeth announced. "It's a bit early, but just a little sherry?"

She bustled behind the counter, her movements efficient and purposeful. Captain immediately followed, I supposed hoping for his own treat.

"The scope of this operation," Freya continued, consulting her research notes, "is pretty much what we already know. But the money kept increasing, and Fletcher needed a way to clean it. I'm not sure how much Edmund knows, but that's when the gang got involved. Fletcher went looking for a referral."

"Surely he knew how dangerous that was," I said, feeling sick at the stupidity of his actions. If he'd been less greedy, we might never have found out, and he might still be alive.

The conversation was interrupted by Captain's sharp yowl from the counter area—not his usual attention-seeking meow, but an urgent warning cry that made all three of us turn immediately.

The ginger tom was positioned beside Ms. Sterling's fresh teacup, back arched, fur standing on end. As we watched, he deliberately knocked the delicate china from the counter, sending it crashing to the floor in a shower of fragments and steaming liquid.

"Captain!" I started to scold, then stopped as I noticed his behavior. This wasn't mischief or clumsiness—this was alarm.

Elspeth hurried over with a tea towel, then froze as she bent to examine the spill. "Good Lord," she breathed. "Something's very wrong with this tea."

The spilled liquid had an odd, oily sheen that caught the afternoon light. More tellingly, the scent was off—overly sweet with bitter undertones that hadn't been present in our earlier cups.

"Don't touch it," Lily said sharply, her face draining of color. "If Captain knocked it over deliberately..."

We stared at the puddle of potentially lethal tea. Captain sat beside it, washing his paws with the satisfied air of a job completed successfully.

"Police," I said, already dialing. "And lock the door— don't let anyone else in."

Elspeth's hands shook as she turned the sign and shot

the bolt. "Someone must have been in my preparation area. While we sat here discussing gangs and money laundering, someone slipped through the back entrance and poisoned that tea."

"How?" Freya whispered. "We would have heard them."

"Not if they were careful." I studied the narrow corridor connecting the main room to the preparation area. "These walls are thick, and we were focused on Freya's news."

"But, someone who knew we'd be here," Lily added. "But why Vivienne?"

The other cups were empty, no slick of oil, all smelling just the way Earl Grey should. Lily was right, this was targeted.

The implications struck home with terrifying clarity. This wasn't panic or desperation—this was the hit man coming to fulfill his contract.

PC Trewin arrived within minutes, followed by DI Drake with a second officer in tow and what appeared to be half the village, drawn by emergency vehicles and the unprecedented sight of Elspeth's tea shop shuttered during business hours.

"Nobody approaches that spill," DI Drake ordered, immediately taking charge of the scene. "I want the building secured and statements from everyone who's been inside today."

"It's been a normal day," Elspeth explained. "No one came in while we were talking. Through the front door anyway. I left the back door off the latch because I expected a delivery."

Dr. Westbrook appeared at the window within minutes. When DI Drake admitted her, the assessment was swift and grim.

"If this is the same foxglove preparation used on Mr.

Fletcher, that dose would have been lethal within hours. Your cat quite literally saved this young woman's life."

Captain preened at the assessment, clearly pleased with his heroic status. Speaking of heroes, I sent a text to Malcolm to keep the corgis with him at the bookshop and that I would explain later.

"This confirms our killer is here," DI Drake announced to the assembled group. "I am sending you to the station to be held in protective custody."

"I am not going to sit in a cell waiting to be safe enough to come home," I said. "I only speak for myself, but I can keep myself safe enough to find this criminal and solve the case."

"I'm going nowhere either," Lily said. "What kind of journalist hides at the climax of the story?"

Ms. Sterling pressed her lips together. I wondered if she was feeling intimidated by our announcements.

"I don't see how locking me away will help," she said. "I want to see this come to an end, so I'll know I'm finally free."

I could almost see the thoughts in DI Drake's mind. She was trying to think of a charge she could arrest us for, but she wasn't having any luck.

"I will leave your protections in place," she said, the words forced through her tight lips. "It means those PCs will not be part of the search for the poisoner."

That was easy to solve. "We will stay together," I said, looking at my fellow potential victims who nodded. "A group is safer and only one PC is needed."

It seemed to satisfy DI Drake who assigned our current protection to stay. She spoke to the PC at the B&B through her radio and had her move into the room with Fitzmoore. Then, turning to the uniformed woman with us, she said, "Do not let them do anything stupid."

She waited until our guard said "Yes, ma'am." And then stormed back on the trail of the hit man.

Freya had been studying the tea shop's configuration. "The back entrance connects to the alley running behind several shops. Perhaps we should wander along to see if there are any footprints, or dropped wallets."

"You need to stay here," our PC said. "Or go to the book-shop. No investigating."

"Just a walk," I said. "You can be with us. Forgive me I don't know your name..."

"PC Burton."

"You'll be there to take anything we might find into official hands. I'm sure you have evidence bags tucked away somewhere."

Her desire to be part of the action warred with her orders. Then she relaxed. "I supposed if you don't wander all over the place, I can protect you."

As we organized ourselves, my phone buzzed with a text from Beau: "Saw emergency vehicles at tea shop. Everything okay? Important client call running long, but can check in after."

The message was quintessentially Beau—concerned but conditional, offering help while explaining why work took priority. Six months ago, I might have appreciated the gesture. Now it simply confirmed what I'd begun to accept about our fundamental incompatibility.

I sent a response to let him know we were fine and not to leave his client hanging.

20

The back lanes were narrow, so tight in fact, that when it came to garbage day, the collectors had to park the truck and wheel out the bins by hand. We wouldn't be able to walk together so we aligned ourselves in a single file. PC Burton dithered about whether the front or rear of the line was the best place to protect us. She settled on the back eventually, it may have had something to do with us all looking at her like she was an idiot.

She muttered, "I can keep a better eye on you from there."

I went first, wishing my brave dogs were with me and not at the bookshop. I thought about what might be a good clue, obviously a dropped wallet with a note inside from whoever hired the hit man would be ideal. Not very likely, though. A signal that someone had hurried past this way, a bottle of poison with DNA and fingerprints.

Whatever waited to be found, I would need to keep my mind clear and my eyes open. We were looking for two people, whoever killed Fletcher and whoever decided to torment us. It didn't feel like they were the same people. A killer would want to get away from suspicion, surely, not sneak around. No one spoke. We concentrated on searching the ground and nooks in the stone walls for anything to help us catch the perpetrator.

At least, that was my goal. I needed this problem solved so I could talk to Beau, and I wouldn't do it with an audience. We'd only made it a few steps when I heard a sigh of exasperation behind me.

"This isn't efficient," Freya said from her position just in front of PC Burton. "We're all looking at the same things. If something is there, surely Ginny will find it before it gets to me."

PC Burton muttered in agreement. "Not the way we would conduct a search."

I wish she would speak up rather than mutter and mumble. Her communication didn't inspire confidence in her abilities. "We can't just stop and talk," I said, "it's too close."

"Let's just take sections," Ms. Sterling said. "Looking at everything is likely to mean we'll miss a clue if it's there. Is that more professional, PC Burton?"

As much as I wanted to find a clue, she was right. I looked directly at PC Burton. "How should we proceed?"

"This is how the force does a search," PC Burton said. "Everything gets double checked, but in sections. Ms. Hampton, you check the ground, I'll do the same. Ms. Sterling and Ms. Ashworth look at the walls. Choose which and focus. Ms. Collins, you are the second pair of eyes on the walls. If you find something, don't touch it. Just speak out."

"That sounds perfect," Freya said. "Please, call me Freya, no need to be formal."

The PC smiled, which softened her face considerably. "If

I was going to be formal, I'd call you Dr. Collins, but that seems a little mean in the circumstances."

Kindness? Or passive aggressive? I could almost hear the southern lady's 'well bless your heart' in her tone. Ms. Sterling's face was stiff with held back emotion. I knew the best way to ease tension was to take action.

"Agreed," I said. "Remember we're looking for the slightest thing. Don't be afraid to point out anything that catches your eye."

To be honest, my optimism was waning fast. Surely a professional wouldn't leave a trace. Then again, they had been foiled by a cat, so perhaps I should be hopeful.

The alley was quite long, normally I suppose it would take a few minutes to walk along, but we were moving at a search party pace. Like on TV when they line up the volunteers and they take a step and look around, side by side.

I turned my attention to the ground, mostly dirt with a few of the original cobblestones still in place. It was well drained so no puddles to hide evidence. At the base of the outside wall, that was as far as I would allow my gaze to travel, clumps of grass and wild plants sprouted. The other wall was the back wall of the various yards we passed. Some of these were better kept than others.

"We should peek inside any of the unlocked yards," Freya said. "Our prey may have hidden to wait out a search."

"We don't have permission," PC Burton said half heartedly.

"No one will mind," Freya said. "We know everyone and none of these people are likely to be happy to abet a killer."

I tried the first door I came to, trusting the others to check what I'd already passed. It was locked. "Any luck?" I asked looked back along the line.

"Only the one, and no indication anyone was inside,"

Lily said. "PC Burton can't check because she needs authorization. I'll be the second eyes on that."

I pointed out a scuff mark with a few blue fibers on the ground and moved along. The next yard didn't have a door. I peeked inside only to find I could see all the way to the street. The newsagent should be much more careful.

"Our poisoner could have walked right through," I reported.

"I'll run in and ask if Mr. Dosanjh saw anyone," Freya called from the back.

"There's a scuff on the wall above the one on the ground," Lily said. "We need to stop so PC Burton can collect evidence."

I turned to watch them, noticing Freya slip into the newsagent's. I didn't know whether to hope the poisoner had escaped to the street or was still dropping clues ahead of us.

"I'm done," PC Burton said as she took her last picture. The two evidence bags went into her pocket.

Freya returned and shook her head. "Good news and bad, I supposed. Mr. Dosanjh said he hadn't noticed someone coming through. He also said he would have seen anyone coming from the back. He's got one of those bead curtains that would have made a racket if anyone passed."

We were about halfway down the alley. By this time our attempted killer would have been confident, and perhaps careless.

Unfortunately, we found nothing else. The alley emptied into a parking lot where delivery trucks would wait for the drivers to return from the shops.

"Don't move," PC Burton ordered as I moved to exit the lot and return to the bookshop.

She was bending over at an empty space. The lot wasn't

paved, just packed pea gravel, but a regular car would have fit in the spot. She peered at the ground and then pulled a pencil from her pocket. Using it to lift something shiny. A ring.

"Stay back," she said as we all crowded in to look at her find. "You'll trample any evidence."

When we moved to a safe distance, she called DI Drake on her radio. "Found something interesting. And I think it narrows down our suspects."

21

W e were told to wait for the DI to arrive and pointed to a space under a large elm in the corner. Still close enough to hear, but far enough to be out of the way of important business.

PC Burton's demeanor had switched from disappointment at her assignment to what definitely looked like pride. Well, she'd found something important so why not.

"Wait for me," DI Drake's voice crackled over the radio.

"What is it?" I called. "Does it mean we're safe? Can we all go about our normal lives?"

She looked at me with that stern but bland expression people in authority use when they don't want to be caught telling a secret.

"You wouldn't have found it if we hadn't looked," Freya said. "Come on, you know DI Drake will tell us."

"That's up to her," PC Burton said. "You should think over your statements."

Of course we'd have to say what we knew. I couldn't think of any other way to cajole the information out of her.

"We shouldn't discuss our statements," I said. "It will taint our testimony if this goes to court."

Freya took a few sheets of paper and pens out of her laptop bag. "We can write notes. Just so we remember what to say."

"Well, the truth," Ms. Sterling said. "I'm done with bending it."

Truth and facts are very different. I gratefully took a sheet of paper and pen from Freya and found a flat section of the wall as a desk. I used bullet points to avoid embellishing. I'd rather be inspecting the ring, but that would come. When I finished, I sent texts to Malcolm and Elliot with our updates. And one to Beau to say I'd probably be late tonight. He didn't acknowledge it.

DI Drake arrived with Trewin and glanced at us as she marched over to PC Burton. They spoke quietly and then I heard her tell PC Trewin to arrange the scene of crime team. "We'll wait here until they come."

Organizing done, she took the evidence bags from PC Burton, gave the ones with the scuff and threads to Trewin and joined us with the ring.

"I can't tell you much," she said. "It does seem like we might have found the identity of the killer, or close enough." She held up the bag. "See this insignia?"

It was a signet ring. One the flat surface used in the past as a wax seal, a circle enclosed a profile of a crow standing on a knife.

"We know this family. My colleagues will find out where everyone involved was at the time of the murder and attempted murder. We'll have this solved by end of day."

Lily leaned in to look closer. "I know who this belongs to," she said. "I did an article about the up and comers in the old gangs."

"You talked to someone like that?" Freya asked, admiration in her tone. "I would never be that brave."

Lily gave a little laugh. "All long distance cameras and listening devices." She glanced at DI Drake. "All approved."

I suppose for an article, anything goes. It's only in cases that go to prosecution that details like search warrants matter. DI Drake didn't say anything, just kept her eyes on Lily.

"Tell her for goodness sake," Ms. Sterling said. "I don't want to be here any longer than necessary. I have a lot of work ahead of me to find new sources of income."

"Sorry," Lily said. "That ring belongs to Freddie McKay. Grandson of George. He thinks he's in line to take over. But the old man thinks he's a fool."

"I know their reputation," DI Drake said. "How do you know this is his?"

"Lots of hours watching him," Lily said. "He taps it on the side of tables when he's meeting people. That dent is a result."

I followed her pointing finger. There was a dent in the gold, very high carat count to be that soft. "So this Freddie, why would he come here to murder a blackmailer, and try to kill one of us?"

"The first I don't know," DI Drake answered. "Perhaps he wanted in and Fletcher told him no."

"What does this man look like?" Ms. Sterling asked.

DI Drake pulled up a photo on her phone. Ms. Sterling gasped. "I saw him on the coastal walk. He must have been trying to stop me from identifying him."

"Only to make it worse. I suppose that's often the case. Getting caught cleaning up," I said. "He'll be easy to catch?"

"The task force is already looking," DI Drake said. "I'll

tell them which McKay is the target. We'll get him talking. I'd prefer it if you all stay around until we have him."

"I can work at the B&B," Lily said. "This is going to be a huge article. What about Fitzmoore?"

"He's still under arrest for his part in the fraud scheme, so nothing will change, but I suppose he isn't the killer." DI Drake called PC Burton over. "You are still on protection duty, but leave Ms. Sterling and Ashworth at the B&B, you are responsible for Ginny and Freya."

PC Burton wasn't happy to be relegated to babysitting us. She pulled herself together and said, "Yes, ma'am."

"Good work, PC. We might never have found this without your diligence. Freddie could have come back and picked up his ring and we would still be running around like idiots."

The praise did its job and PC Burton led us back to the bookshop after dropping off the two tour participant at Mrs. Pengelly's B&B.

22

I t only took an hour to locate Freddie McKay, surprising all of us. Lily and Ms. Sterling, I couldn't quite make myself think of her as Viviene—too long a way from doctor to first name basis, had been called to the makeshift police station. Fitzmoore was still under room arrest, Malcolm and Freya were running the bookshop. Since that left just a small group, I'd be responsible for updating everyone.

DI Drake pointed to the chairs set up on the side of the hall. There was a table set up as if we were attending a private lecture. The main difference was the two rather tough-looking men standing behind a younger man attempting to appear unconcerned. The sweat dripping from his hairline told us far more than his slouch.

"My colleagues from London," DI Drake said. "DIs John Hawke and Mickey Right. And here we have Freddie McKay, erstwhile gangster and attempted poisoner."

He gave us a lazy grin, another attempt at arrogance. "Alleged."

Why he'd agreed to let us sit in on the interrogation was

more puzzling than DI Drake's invitation. Perhaps we were to be used as some kind of technique. Facing his potential victims.

"Freddie, we have you dead to rights," DI Hawke said, his voice gravelly as if he'd taken a jab to his throat.

"And your granddad is not happy with you," DI Right added. "Just remember you'll have to face him even when you're a guest of his majesty's."

Freddie paled and sat straighter. "Just trying to bring in business. I should be taking over the family when the old man kicks it. Gotta show him I can do it."

Ah. And now he might have spoiled his chances of inheriting control of the McKay enterprise.

"You agreed to tell us everything," DI Drake said. "We have a deal. You give us useful information, and we reduce your charges."

"Yeah, it's going to take me some time to be the grass you want. You know the code, no talking." The smug grin between Hawke and Right told me there was far more to the deal than just a trade of prison time.

DI Right gave Freddie a nudge. "We all know that code only lasts for about five minutes after an arrest. Get on with it."

Freddie pursed his lips reminding me of a two-year-old who didn't want to eat his Brussels sprouts.

"Right. So, I heard about this guy, pulling a scam, right? Came to me for advice on cleaning the profits. Thought it would be something the family would like. Pretty easy to do, no need to beat anyone up."

Fletcher. We knew he'd been looking at money laundering.

DI Hawke glared at Freddie. "Keep going, no need for dramatic pauses."

Freddie had settled enough to give him a glare. "Yeah, well when I told him I wanted a piece, he said his partner wouldn't like it. Told him maybe he only needs one partner. The kind with useful contacts."

I felt Lily shift next to me and glanced across. She was filling a notebook with some form of shorthand. Ms. Sterling was rigid. I suppose if you are the potential victim, Freddie's story might feel less interesting and more horrifying.

"He said he'd think about it," Freddie continued. "Didn't take him long. Called me in but not to do the partner, he thought there was a witness. Someone who could put him in the frame. Idiot should have left it to the pros."

The timing seemed quite wrong. I coughed to get DI Drake's attention. "May I ask a questions, just to move this along?"

"Fine," she said and turned back to watch Freddie.

"I thought, we thought, you killed Mr. Fletcher, but that's not the case?"

He rolled his eyes, and I realized he was a kid, no more than eighteen or nineteen. What an awful start to his life.

"You thought wrong. I expected to get the call to off Fletcher, but he was already dead. I came down to killer her." He pointed at Ms. Sterling. "I didn't ask what she saw. She was a problem and I wanted the business. End of."

"Your contact was Edmund?" Lily asked.

"Yeah, that Fitzmoore guy," Freddie said.

DI Drake nodded and waved a hand at her colleagues. "I suppose that's all we need, gentlemen. Take him away."

The handcuffs went on despite Freddie's attempt to wiggle out of it. "Granddad won't be happy."

DI Right laughed. "He told us you'd benefit from some time inside. You can always get a better deal by grassing on him instead of someone lower in the chain. Maybe no time inside, a new identity."

"I might be a grass, but I'm not suicidal," Freddie muttered as he was led out to the waiting car.

DI Drake took in a deep breath. "Thank you. We knew he was holding something back and we couldn't get him to tell us."

"You thought having us in the room might make him cocky," Lily said. "Good tactic."

"He's not the brightest bulb, but loyalty—fear—is powerful in his world. Yes, three innocent looking women made him want to brag."

"Where did you find him?" I thought it was odd that he didn't run back to London where he could hide.

"He's the squatter at the grounds keeper's cottage. He said he was going to try again. Make sure no cats were around." DI Drake dusted her hands together. "Now we need to get Fitzmoore to confess to more than a little financial crime. I'm afraid Freddie McKay's testimony isn't enough."

23

Before we jumped into the planning phase of the trap, I needed to make sure we wouldn't be side tracked. The two men in my life were wonderful, but I didn't think they would agree to such a risky operation. Time to give them jobs so they wouldn't get into danger.

Elliot was my first call, because if he was busy with veterinarian duties, I would need a plan B for the corgis—perhaps Mrs. Pengelly?

"I'd be delighted," Elliot said. "They can accompany me on a couple of calls. I promise I'll return both Hardy and Austen tired, happy, and clean."

I thanked him and told him where to pick them up, while imagining Austen and Hardy trotting around a farm yard attempting to make the animals obey orders. Better for Elliot to be in charge.

My next call was to Beau. If he didn't answer I would have to go to the cottage to speak to him in person. And that's what happened. Voicemail. I didn't bother to leave a message. PC Burton escorted me the short walk and waited discreetly outside.

Beau was ending a call as I walked into the kitchen. He'd taken over every surface with printouts and dirty mugs. I didn't comment because I knew he'd clean up when he was finished. I had no idea what his new company did that involved so many crises, and globally at that, but he was the right person for the job.

"Ginny!" he said coming toward me for a hug. "I know this has been a terrible visit. I promise to be more attentive."

I updated him on the situation. Not the details, but the facts. We'd caught Freddie, received information that will close the case and needed him to stay at the cottage. "Minimize the risks," I said without elaborating.

"When you write your memoir, it will be exciting," he said. "I think I can manage to stay here, but tonight, we should celebrate."

His phone buzzed. Even when giving me a hug it was in his hand. I glanced at the screen and read, Jakarta Client - EMERGENCY.

He did give me an apologetic look before answering and turning his back to me. I was surprised at how little his action hurt.

"Morrison here. What's the situation?" His entire demeanor shifted into high-alert business mode. "When did this happen? How much are we talking about? No, I understand, this is the kind of crisis that requires personal attention."

He hung up and started packing all his paperwork in this computer bag. "This big deal in Jakarta deal is collapsing." He looked at the dishes spread around as he packed the laptop. "I'll take care of this."

"Don't worry about it. I can clear up later," I said. "Do you need to leave immediately?"

"As soon as I can," he gave me a peck on the cheek. "I don't suppose I need a police escort to head to the station?"

Why didn't I feel anything? I suppose the answer was in the question. This is how Beau Morrison worked. I called PC Burton into the kitchen and asked about Beau's safety.

She used the radio to call DI Drake. We all heard the answer. "He's not on the list. I don't know if our perp even knows who he is."

"Ah, then I'm glad to be somewhat anonymous. My assistant is booking me on the earliest flight in the morning. I'll take the train to the airport. I'll call you when I can. Good luck."

I accepted his kiss on the cheek and told him to leave his spare key with Dot next door. I suppose I'd done the same to him, if I'm honest. He'd been absorbed in his work, I'd been focused on the investigation. Perhaps the emotion I should be feeling is embarrassment that I'd blamed him for abandoning me, when I was as guilty. Of course, I hadn't shown up out of the blue for a visit.

24

W hen we returned to the town hall, I joined everyone at the table where DI Drake placed an open folder with copies of documents inside. I'd called and told Malcolm and Freya to close the shop and join us as we crossed the green. While we waited a PC I hadn't met yet, put on the kettle and opened a package of chocolate digestives.

"The trap," DI Drake said as soon as we updated our two new arrivals, "needs to make Edmund believe we have evidence he doesn't know about. Something that directly links him to the murder, not just the fraud."

"What kind of evidence?" I asked. I wondered if there was a handbook for these situations. A list of acceptable traps for criminals. There must be something because getting a sting together so quickly without a system was impossible.

"Backup files from Tobias," Lily suggested. "Documents he kept as insurance against Edmund's betrayal. Financial records, correspondence, even recordings of their conversations about the murder."

DI Drake nodded approvingly. "Perfect. Edmund knows Tobias was paranoid about documentation. The idea that he kept murder insurance files would be entirely believable. But Tobias didn't know about Fitzmoore's meeting with Freddie. We'll give some thought to those recording. I suspect they will be the juiciest bait. "

"Where would these supposed files be hidden?" Malcolm asked with the focus that made him invaluable to investigations and rare books collectors.

"The bookshop," I said. "Hampton's Books has already been broken into twice, but Edmund doesn't know the extent of that search. We can claim Freya discovered a hidden cache while helping me reorganize after the investigation. Just Freya, Malcolm, and I. No need to crowd the room."

"Brilliant," Freya said, practically bouncing in her chair. "I can create a completely plausible backstory. The story is easy, Tobias was paranoid that Edmund wouldn't stay loyal, kept backup evidence in case their partnership soured. Left a note with it when he broke in saying if anything happens to him, we should know the details."

DI Drake was making rapid notes. "That's excellent. Edmund would believe Tobias capable of that level of preparation. But we need more than just files—we need something that directly threatens him."

"That's where the recordings come in," Lily said. "Secret recordings of Edmund discussing the murder with Freddie. Tobias followed him to London. Planned to confront him but got murdered first?"

"It doesn't explain why he'd drink tea with Edmund," I said. "In fact, it undermines the case. If Tobias heard the murder plan, then he'd avoid his partner."

That was the crux. Recordings would draw Edmund, but

any defense barrister would jump on the conflict. "What if the recordings simply proved Edmund was in charge?" I asked. I was still thinking it through and hoped one of the others would fill in the rest.

Lily practically bounced in her seat. "Yes, he recorded the money laundering part, but that's all. I'm not sure that he'll expect details, but it's good to have just in case."

"What if he wants to listen to the audio?" I asked. "He won't be eager to confess all as if he's a Bond villain."

DI Drake smiled at that. "We'll have it somewhere. Freddie has been under surveillance for a long time. We'll get the date from him, pull the recordings."

"Perfect," Malcolm said, adjusting his bow tie with particular satisfaction. "Nothing terrifies a killer more than their own voice confirming their guilt."

"There's one problem," I said. "If we're claiming these files contain evidence of Edmund committing murder, why haven't we turned them over to the police immediately?"

"Because," Freya said with growing excitement, "I only found them last night. Late, after everyone had gone home. I was helping Ginny reorganize the storage room, found the package in a file."

Ms. Sterling touched the papers DI Drake had. "I can do a better job than this."

DI Drake called the PC over. "Give Ms. Sterling access to whatever she needs."

"Why would he leave this with us?" Malcolm asked. "Why not have it sent to the police."

"Because Tobias knew you'd investigate it," Lily said. "That you would read the information and then give it to the police. And if nothing happened to him, he could easily retrieve the package during one of our visits."

The plan sounded perfect. Edmund would absolutely

believe Tobias capable of that level of manipulation and forward planning.

"How will Edmund find out about this?" I asked. "It's all well and good to make the perfect trap, but we need him to hear the evidence has been found, and to come to the bookshop. He needs to escape his guards."

"Easy enough," Lily said. "Viv and I will accidentally talk about it outside his door. DI Drake, you need to make an opportunity for him to slip out and go after the bait."

"Easily done," she said. "The PC can leave his room now we've taken Freddie into custody. He can go back to guarding from the kitchen. If we didn't know Fitzmoore was the killer, we wouldn't lock him down so tightly."

"So, when will we put this into action?" I needed to make sure Elliot knew when it would be safe to bring back Austen and Hardy.

"Three hours?" Freya said. "The store will just be closing. It won't be odd that we're still there. And no customers will be in danger."

Malcolm consulted his pocket watch. "That's quite achievable. In fact, any longer and the village gossip line will have all the details, and we'll be risking Mr. Fitzmoore learning it's a trap."

"What about the actual goal, getting his confession recorded?" I asked. "How do we safely document Edmund's confession without anyone getting hurt?"

DI Drake's expression grew serious. "That's where police work takes over. Luckily, his room faces away from the shop. We'll set up equipment quite discreetly. We'll be listening in. When we have what we need, we'll come in. If it sounds like you aren't safe, we'll come in. If you want us to come before that, just ask for help."

"He's already tried poisoning once," Freya pointed out calmly. "We should assume he'll plan something."

The thought of Edmund in my bookshop with deadly poison made my hands shake slightly as I reached for my teacup. But if it was the only way to get justice for Tobias, then we had to try.

"One final question," I said as we reviewed the complete plan. "What if Edmund doesn't take the bait? What if he decides to run instead of trying to destroy evidence?"

"Then we track him down and arrest him for the fraud and work on getting the evidence solid enough on the murder," DI Drake said simply. "But I don't think he'll run. His entire life is here—his business, his reputation. Running would be admitting failure."

I returned to Hampton Books. Lily, Freya, and Ms. Sterling remained in the town hall preparing our bait.

It took an hour to set up the bookshop for capturing our killer. Listening devices in place, pathways cleared to allow the police to enter. I glanced around and couldn't see any of the surveillance equipment even though I'd watched every installation.

Now my bookshop was transformed into an elaborate trap for a desperate killer. The comfortable chairs had been moved to allow for sight-lines and the entire space thrummed with hidden technology.

"One final briefing," DI Drake said, gathering us around Malcolm's tea service for what might be our last peaceful conversation before confronting a murderer. "Edmund Fitzmoore is desperate, intelligent, and has already demonstrated willingness to kill. He will not surrender easily."

"Understood," Freya said with determination. "We'll be very careful."

"Ms. Sterling and Ms. Ashford should be starting their

parts soon," Malcolm said as he consulted his pocket watch. "That leaves whatever time Edmund takes to make his escape. Let's hope it doesn't mean hours. I admit I'm eager to get this over with and go back to normal."

"We're watching him," DI Drake added. "As soon as he takes a step toward the bookshop, we'll move into place."

It didn't take more than thirty minutes. My heart pounded as I stood in the shadows of the office doorway and watched Edmund, checking for observers before trying the front door. Finding it unlocked he slipped inside, holding up a hand to silence the chime.

25

I held my breath, a cliche, I know, but all the same. We were all in place, me in the office doorway, Malcolm in a nook behind the mystery section, Freya at the foot of the stairs to the second floor and her apartment above. The dogs safely with Elliot, Captain was my only worry. He had a strong protective streak and wandered where he chose.

If all went well, I would come out of the office and be surprised by finding Edmund. He'd end up confession all. And then we'd return to our normal lives. Selling books, gossiping about strangers in the tabloids, and eating too many scones.

I wasn't naive enough to think all would go well. I'd settle for no one getting hurt. When we planned it, the trap felt perfect, now I was in the middle of it, I couldn't believe I'd agreed or that DI Drake had approved.

When we set the bait, the fabricated papers had looked convincing in the lamplight—names, payment records, correspondence about degree verifications. A CD with a transcript of Edmund talking to Freddie—actually real thanks to the diligence of the task force. They'd scrubbed through the surveillance recordings for the day and found what we needed.

Unfortunately, DI Drake told us Edmund could explain it away and gangsters didn't make reliable witnesses. And the part about killing his partner was removed based on our earlier concerns.

While I'd been second guessing everything, Edmund had made a circuit of the reading area. Why, I had no idea. The important part was that he stopped at the table with evidence and took the chair, it was all I could do to let out my breath without a whoosh.

We were off comms. That's what DI Drake called it. No hidden earpiece, no whispered instructions. I knew my role and would trust that others knew theirs. And that the planted devices were working.

I was about to step out and being my surprise act when Edmund turned toward where I was apparently not as well hidden as I'd thought.

"Working rather late, aren't you, Ginny?" Edmund asked, his voice cold. "And in the dark. Is that normal? Your little uniformed escort has left you unprotected and there's a murderer in the village. The police just don't know how to do their jobs, do they?"

"The gangster is in custody," I replied, hoping he wouldn't notice the tremor in my voice. "We are all safe now. I was just getting ready to leave. I tend to turn off the lights when no one is here."

He kept scanning the papers on the desk. "You should lock your door after hours," he said. "Even in a sleepy little village like this. You never know who's passing through."

I reached for the light switch. Being in the dark wasn't making this easy. "On the way out," I said. "I lock it when I leave."

He made a little grunt, like people do when they don't want to agree or argue. He turned to look at me and waved his hand toward the evidence. "This is interesting. Is there more?"

"I have no idea what Tobias did to protect himself," I said. "That is all he left here. I was about to pack it up and take it to the police."

"Where did you find it?"

The whole conversation was bizarre. I suppose I should be happy he wasn't overtly threatening, but in his presence, I could only describe his attitude as creepy. I was under no illusion he wouldn't lash out. I reminded myself of my goal. To get him to confess. "At some point he must have slipped into my office. We found it cleaning up after the break in."

He nodded like he accepted the story. "I thought you had something on me," he said. "That's why I searched your files. I missed it. Didn't think Tobias was that smart."

"Is it true?" I asked. "I thought Fletcher made it up to frame you. That's why I haven't given it to DI Drake yet."

"What exactly does this add up to?" he asked. His composure cracked. We had him worried.

"Tobias was thorough. I'm not sure how he got most of this information," I said. "The scheme was definitely larger in scope than you led us to believe. Your entire partnership, Edmund. Every transaction, every credential sold, every payment received. The main difference is it all points to you as the instigator, not Tobias Fletcher as you led us to believe."

The silence stretched as Edmund studied the evidence. Then he turned to me. "I'm afraid I can't allow you to share that information with your pet DI. You really are arrogant. I supposed it's part of being American. Normal people don't try to beat the police to solve even a petty crime."

That stung. He was right, my competitiveness was a big part of the reason I followed clues. The fact he'd bought the whole trap was a relief, though.

"What are you going to do?" I suddenly remembered we were recording this whole interaction. I needed him to confess with no doubt. How would I start him talking?

"Deal with a nosy bookseller and then run. I can move my money before the police freeze the accounts. Find a nice sunny place with no extradition." His voice had changed—gone flat.

"They haven't already—frozen your funds? But you were arrested for fraud." Was he delusional or had something slipped through the cracks?

"I made some arrangements before coming" He pulled a foldable tote from his pocket and shook it open. "It will take them a while to find the new accounts. The balances will be zero before they do."

He picked up the CD and transcript and dropped them into the bag.

"Are you sure?" I hoped DI Drake was on the radio ordering someone to find the money fast.

"Yes." He picked up several of the documents and tapped them so they fell into a neat stack. These followed the CD and transcript. "I'm sorry this has to end this way. You won't have a chance to implement any of the lesson you've learned about dealing with killers."

He didn't have a gun, so I wasn't in immediate danger. If he thought I would drink or eat in his presence, he was an idiot. "Is Freddie right? We have him, you know."

"Ah, Freddie. He doesn't stand up to the McKay name, does he?"

The evidence was all in the bag now. "When did you plan to kill Tobias?"

"I suppose you've earned some answers," he said. "Sit and I'll tell you everything. Perhaps over a nightcap?"

I waited for him to take a chair before obeying. "I think I'll pass on a drink, Thanks"

He nodded his head slowing as if agreeing with my caution. "Understandable, but not the obstacle you think."

I can't explain how disconcerting this was. Talking politely, feeling the menacing subtext, and still not running for help.

"At first it was all fine. I had a nice sideline. The institutions created the market, you know. Making it difficult and expensive the get credentials. Then I suppose the industry added to it. I mean really why do so many jobs require a PhD?"

"So it was a service?" I asked. Maybe pretending I agreed with him would get him spilling the confession. "Filling a gap in the market?"

"Exactly," Edmund replied with the conviction of someone who'd rationalized his crimes completely. "And people need to eat, after all."

I found his twisted logic both fascinating and horrifying. In Edmund's mind, he wasn't defrauding the system—he was reforming it.

"Tell me about your partnership with Tobias," I pressed, gesturing to the fake documents he was holding. "How did it really work?"

Edmund's composure cracked further. "Tobias Fletcher discovered my operation eighteen months ago—pure accident while researching potential blackmail targets. He found one of my clients and traced the credentials back to me."

"So he blackmailed you?" Was that at least true?

"Initially, yes. Five thousand pounds to keep quiet about

the fraud operation. But Tobias was too clever for simple extortion." Edmund's voice grew bitter with remembered betrayal. "He convinced me we could be partners—his research skills identifying potential clients, my expertise creating the credentials they needed. It seemed... mutually beneficial."

"What went wrong?" I suspected we all knew the answer.

"Greed. Control. Tobias wanted everything—fifty percent of profits, final approval over all clients, expansion into international markets." Edmund's hands clenched into fists. "He was treating our service like a corporate enterprise rather than a mission to help deserving people. The literary tour was supposed to be a recruitment opportunity, a chance for him to identify new victims for his blackmail schemes. Instead it was filled with current clients."

"So you killed him," I asked. Surely that wasn't entrapment. It seemed like the logical question.

"I protected everything he was threatening to destroy," Edmund corrected, his voice carrying a righteous indignation. "He hinted that if he didn't get his way, he'd send evidence to the police and cut a deal for turning me in."

"Wouldn't it have been better to simply find some halfway point? A bit of expansion, but not as much as he wanted?"

"He wouldn't have stopped," Edmund said. "The best option was to close up shop—open somewhere else, but first he had to be out of the picture."

"Tell me about his last moments," I asked, not because I wanted to know, but the confession couldn't leave any questions.

He looked at the bag, which was lying at his feet. Then

at me. I saw the decision on his face. He wanted to brag and since he planned on killing me, there was no downside.

"I went to his room that evening to discuss his demands one final time. Behaved like I was going to agree. Told him we should celebrate our partnership properly." Edmund's voice grew distant with memory. "While he was in the bathroom, I put the foxglove in his tea."

"Why foxglove?"

"Do you think I walk around with poison at hand? It was the only thing growing in that woman's garden that I knew how to use."

"It sounds like you planned this before you got here," I said. "Why didn't you come prepared?"

He gave me a look that said he thought I was too stupid to understand. "And leave a trail? Have my face recorded procuring a deadly poison?"

"I wouldn't know how that works," I said. "Didn't Tobias suspect?"

"Why would he? We'd been drinking tea, talking business." Edmund's cold attitude couldn't quite mask the satisfaction in his voice. "The foxglove is virtually tasteless when you put it in flavored tea. He drank the entire cup while explaining his expansion plans. That recording doesn't contain our discussion about changing partners, do it?"

"And then you left," I said. I felt no obligation to answer his questions.

"Long enough to make sure he was showing symptoms, yes. Told him I needed time to consider his proposals, that we'd finalize everything in the morning." Edmund's precision was horrifying. "I was safely back in my room when the symptoms became obvious."

The complete confession—fraud operation, murder method, timeline, motive. Everything DI Drake needed for prosecution. Why wasn't the store filled with uniformed police? What had I missed?

Edmund wasn't finished.

"Of course, I can't allow you to share any of this information with Detective Inspector Drake," he said, his tone becoming conversational. "Particularly not with these files as evidence."

"Edmund, the police already suspect you killed him, thanks to Freddie," I said, though I could hear uncertainty creeping into my voice. "Killing me won't change anything."

"It will eliminate the most damaging witness and destroy the most incriminating evidence," Edmund replied with terrifying calm. "Without your testimony and these documents, they have only circumstantial evidence about my business arrangements. Fraud won't be a priority."

He reached into his pocket and pulled out a small glass bottle. The kind Victorian apothecaries used to dispense tinctures.

"I brought the same foxglove preparation I used on Tobias," he said. "Remarkably effective when properly administered. You'll simply appear to have suffered a heart attack while working late, poor Ginny never taking a break."

The casual way he discussed my murder made it clear this wasn't desperate improvisation. Edmund had planned this possibly as soon as he realized he might have let something slip.

That's when Captain decided he'd heard enough and stood up on his shelf, stretched with deliberate feline authority, and knocked over an entire stack of poetry volumes. The books tumbled to the floor with a tremendous crash that echoed through the shop like a cannon shot.

Edmund spun toward the sound, startled. "What the devil—?"

"Time to end this charade," Malcolm said, stepping around a bookcase.

"And time for the authorities to step in," I said.

Edmund looked around the shop, frantically looking for an escape route. Freya joined us and he must have realize there was no way out.

"You recorded me," he said, more statement than question.

"Every word," I confirmed. "DI Drake has everything she needs."

The front door opened as DI Drake and her officers entered. No dramatic confrontation with battering rams and everyone shouting orders, no violence—just the inevitable conclusion of a plan that had worked exactly as intended.

"Edmund Fitzmoore," DI Drake said, "you're under arrest for the murder of Tobias Fletcher and the attempted murder of Vivienne Sterling." She read him his rights as Edmund stared at her open-mouthed.

Edmund looked at the bottle in his hand—the poison that would have killed another innocent person—me. For a moment, I thought he might drink the contents himself. Instead, he set it carefully on the table.

"I was trying to protect them," he said as the handcuffs clicked into place. "All those people who trusted me. Their lives are ruined now."

I didn't believe his sudden change. This man had no empathy. He was trying to protect his income stream.

"You protected a criminal enterprise by committing murder," DI Drake replied. "The people who trusted you were victims of fraud, not beneficiaries of reform."

As Edmund was led away, I realized how quiet the bookshop had become. The only sounds were Captain's satisfied purring and the gentle sound of Malcolm and Freya returning the poetry books to their shelves.

"Outstanding work," DI Drake said, examining the poison bottle and recording equipment. "We have everything—complete confession to the whole operation, detailed admission of murder method, and attempted assault with the same poison. And his fingerprints and DNA will be all over this bottle. The Crown Prosecution Service will have no trouble with this case."

"What about the credential fraud victims?" Malcolm asked. "Eight hundred people face losing their positions."

"We call them victims, but don't forget, they committed fraud too. Using what they knew were fraudulent degrees is not the act of an innocent person. The cases will be reviewed individually. I suspect they'll get off with probation and a fine. The damage to their reputations will be punishment enough."

"Ms. Sterling?" I asked. "She seemed genuinely knowledgeable despite the false credentials."

"I think she'll find her feet somewhere," DI Drake said. "At least Ms. Ashworth wasn't part of the enterprise. Her article may win her a journalist award."

As the police finished collecting evidence and removing equipment, I found myself alone in the bookshop with Malcolm and Freya—Captain had disappeared after all the excitement.

But Hampton's Books had survived another investigation, and our community was safe.

26

The excitement of the case lingered for a few days on the village gossip line, but the rumor of a royal visit to our area had replaced murder and fraud. A week after the arrest, DI Drake sent me an email saying that since I was a witness and would be called to testify, she couldn't give me any update. But her email ended with a thumbs up emoji.

Beau was still on his world tour of crisis management with not one contact since he left. I tried not to feel the fool for thinking this time would be different.

At the end of a busy day, I started the closing routine, Malcolm had offered to stay and let me go home early, so I only did the minimum. Oliver's latest idea was sitting on the counter beside the cash register. Murder mystery evenings. I'd already told him I wasn't interested. What I didn't say was that if he wanted to bring in tourists, he could do the work. It seemed a little unnecessary.

The door chimed, and I expected a late browser. When I looked up, Elliot stepped in to my line of sight carrying a bottle of champagne.

"I hope I'm not presuming," he said, "but I thought we might celebrate the quiet between murders." He smiled as he said it making it clear he was joking.

"Champagne is always welcome," I said. "I don't have any flutes."

He brought his hand from behind his back to reveal two appropriate glasses. "Are you free for dinner?"

I didn't say always, or what took you so long. I said, "I'd like that very much." I had no idea why our budding relationship came to a halt, but it did seem like he'd been avoiding me since the arrest, and I was glad he'd come.

We settled on the pub, walking distance and the dogs were welcome as long as they didn't roam around. And it was everything I hoped an English pub would be when I decided to move to Devon. A warm fire in a huge fireplace that looked to be a few hundred years old. Dark beams, cream walls, and a bar that went from one wall to the other. The buzz of conversation was comforting, and the beer was perfect. Best of all, they served fish and chips.

We ordered and settled in with our drinks. Elliot straightened and became quite serious.

"I need to tell you something that I should have said weeks ago," he began. "I stepped back because I thought the honorable thing was to let you choose between us without pressure. But that was cowardice disguised as courtesy."

"Elliot—"

"Let me finish," he said. His nerves showing as he fiddled with the beer mat. "I realized something during the investigation. When that madman threatened you, when you were in actual danger, my first instinct wasn't to be noble or patient. It was to make sure you were safe, whatever it took."

My heart was racing now. "And?"

"And I realized that's what matters. Not grand gestures or complicated history, but whether someone's first thought is about your wellbeing." He leaned closer, close enough that I could see the fine lines around his eyes, the result of years spent squinting into bright Devon sunlight. "Mine always is."

"I know," I said softly. "I noticed."

His posture relaxed with my words. "Did you? Good. Because I'm done being patient. I want to be with you, Ginny. I want to be part of whatever comes next—the investigations, the adventures, the quiet evenings reading in that cottage of yours with the dogs sprawled across our feet."

"Our feet?"

"Well, I'm rather hoping you'll let me stick around for the long term," he said with a smile that made my chest tight. "Assuming you're interested in having a vet in your life. I may not be jetting around the world, but I have never figured out how to get farm animals to need my services during office hours. I also happen to be completely in love with you."

I reached for his hands, marveling at how right they felt in mine. "I am interested," I said carefully. "Very interested."

"Excellent," he said, and kissed me.

It was nothing like the dramatic embraces in the romance novels we sold, but it was perfect for us—honest, warm, and full of promise. When we broke apart, I felt like something that had been out of alignment for months had finally clicked into place.

"So," Elliot said, his arms still around me, "shall we make this official? Dating, courting, whatever you'd like to call it?"

"I'd like that very much," I said. "It would be nice if

crime passed Tidehaven on it's way somewhere else, but you do know I won't sit back if someone dies under mysterious circumstance."

"I don't plan on changing you, Ginny. I hope you'd let me help in future," he said.

That was good to hear. "I will do my best to include you. No need to reciprocate. I have no interest in helping you on farms."

Our dinners arrived with a smile from our waitress. Elsie something who loved to read racy romances. "About time, Dr. Harrington. The entire village was betting on you two."

The meal passed in companionable silence while we enjoyed the excellent fish and chips.

"Will you be asked to testify?" he asked after ordering a shared dessert of local fruit and cheeses. I'd been won over to this delicacy in my first week.

"Yes. It won't be for a while. The justice system doesn't move at a rapid pace. So will Ms. Sterling, Lily, Freya, and Malcolm. Although it's always possible Edmund will plead guilty if they can get him a good enough deal."

"Speaking of your fellow crime fighters," Elliot said, reaching for another scone, "there's something you should know. Ms. Sterling stopped by the clinic yesterday."

I knew she'd decided to stay in the area and concentrate on getting her credentials the old-fashioned way. Freya was helping her through the process of applying for and earning work experience credits. "Oh? How is she settling in?"

"Very well, actually. She's found a cottage to let on the other side of the village and wants to make Tidehaven Cove her permanent home. Came in and asked if I could help her adopt a puppy." He paused to dip a slice of cheese in a pool of dark honey. "She also mentioned that she's been helping

Malcolm authenticate some unusual items that have turned up in your rare collection. For her thesis."

This was the first I'd heard of them working together. "What kind of unusual items?"

"A collection of Medieval manuscripts, apparently, from an estate sale. Fragments that suggest there might be a much larger collection hidden somewhere locally." His eyes twinkled with mischief. "The sort of thing that would interest someone who's become known for solving book-related mysteries."

"Like a treasure hunt. That will make Malcolm happy." And how could that go wrong?

Elliot reached across the table to take my hand. "Don't feel you only have to investigate murders, Ginny. A good treasure hunt can be fun and much less dangerous."

I laughed. "As long as the treasure is musty old documents?"

27

Three weeks after Elliot and I became officially a couple, Hampton's Books had transformed from a crime scene back into the heart of Tidehaven Cove's literary community. We'd added a little more security, not intrusive, but enough to keep out a casual attempt, and record anyone who did manage to break in. All very subtle but significant—new deadbolts on all entrances, a professional security system that Malcolm had insisted upon.

"We've had enough break ins, and we know gangsters aren't staying in the city," he'd said.

I refrained from reminding him how appalled he was when I brought in the iPad to replace the ancient card impression machine.

I was checking our morning deliveries when Malcolm called me to the front. There, to my surprise and Malcolm's distaste by his expression, stood Beau Morrison. Looking every inch the successful publishing executive but carrying the slightly hollow expression of someone who'd been living on caffeine and conference calls.

"Ginny," he said, setting down his travel bag. "I hope you

don't mind me dropping by. I fly back to New York tonight, but I wanted to talk before I left."

"Of course," I said, noting how different he looked compared to three weeks ago. Success suited him, but it also seemed to have carved away something essential. It was out of his way to come to Tidehaven, so this must be important to him. "How did the Jakarta negotiation go?"

"Better than expected. The deal's closed, and they've offered me the senior partnership." His smile was proud but tired. "It's everything I've worked toward for the past decade."

Malcolm emerged from the back room carrying the second best version of our tea service. "Congratulations on your achievement, Mr. Morrison. Tea?"

"Please," Beau said gratefully, settling into one of our reading chairs.

I poured while Beau looked around the shop, taking in the security improvements and new displays. When I handed him his cup, he met my eyes with the kind of direct honesty that had first attracted me to him years ago.

"I need to tell you something, Ginny. About why I'm really here." He took a sip as if to fortify himself.

Since Elliot and I had settled into a solid relationship, I didn't worry that Beau would fool me again with this good intentions. "Go on."

"The partnership comes with a move. I'd be heading their new London office, overseeing European acquisitions. It means relocating permanently, building an entirely new division from the ground up." He paused, stirring his tea slowly. "It's a five-year commitment, probably longer."

I felt something settle inside me—not disappointment, or not much of it. "That's incredible, Beau. You must be thrilled."

"I am," he said, and I could hear the surprise in his voice. "That's what I needed to tell you. Three weeks ago, when they first mentioned this possibility, my immediate thought was about how it would affect us. How I could make it work with spending time here, with trying to rebuild what we had."

"And now?"

"Now I realize I was kidding myself." He set down his teacup with careful precision. "When the crisis hit and they needed someone in Jakarta immediately, I didn't hesitate. Didn't even think about asking them to send someone else. I was on a plane six hours later."

"That's who you are, Beau," I said gently. "It's what makes you brilliant at what you do."

"It's also what makes me a terrible boyfriend," he replied with rueful honesty. "You deserve someone whose first instinct is to protect you, not someone who gets excited about international crises because they represent career opportunities."

The relief I felt was immediate and complete. "Yes, we want different things from life."

"We do. And there's nothing wrong with either of our choices." He gestured around the shop, where morning light streamed through windows that now featured discrete security sensors. "Look at what you've built here. This community trusts you, relies on you. You've become someone who makes a real difference in people's lives."

"While you've become someone who makes things happen on an international scale," I countered. "We've both found where we belong."

"There's something else I want to say," Beau said as our conversation wound down. "About Elliot."

My cheeks warmed. "What about him?"

"I may have been distracted by work, but I wasn't blind. The way he looked at you during the investigation, the way he positioned himself to protect you without making a fuss about it." Beau's smile was genuinely warm. "He's exactly what you need, Ginny. Someone whose first priority is the people he cares about."

"Beau—"

"I'm not saying this to be noble," he interrupted. "I'm saying it because it's true. He sees who you are now, not who you used to be. And more importantly, he wants to be part of this life you've built, not drag you away from it."

I told him that I knew exactly what he meant. That a year ago in my old life, I would have laughed at anyone who suggested I'd slow down, even take a weekend off. And yet, here I was in a sleepy smuggler's village in Devon. Surrounded by people with eccentricities, and warm hearts. Running a bookshop with a young woman full of life and an older man who held every rule as a comfort blanket.

To his credit, Beau hugged me when I told him about Elliot and I being together.

After Beau left, running for the train as usual, I stood in the shop absorbing the finality of our conversation. Years of friendship, and a few months of trying to be more, had taught us both the same lesson. We were exactly where we should be.

"That went well," Freya said, emerging from the back room where she'd been updating our online inventory. "Not that I was eavesdropping."

I chuckled. "It did, you can spread the news as wide as you want," I replied.

∾

Ginny inherits a rare book collection. Will the other heirs be happy for her?
Grab your copy of Inheritance of Ill Will here.

Claim your copy of The Charleston Diary when you sign up for my newsletter. Learn how Ginny solved a case of forgery before she headed to the peace and tranquility of Tidehaven Cove.

CLICK HERE

If you enjoyed reading Poison and Prose please consider helping other readers to find the story by leaving a review. Click here to review.

WANT MORE

Ginny inherits a rare book collection. Will the other heirs be happy for her?

Use the QR code to grab your copy of Inheritance of Ill Will.

FREE BOOK

Use the QR code to claim your copy of The Charleston Diary when you sign up for my newsletter. Learn how Ginny solved a case of forgery before she headed to the peace and tranquility of Tidehaven Cove.

REVIEW

If you enjoyed reading Poison and Prose please consider helping other readers to find the story by using the QR code to leave a review.

ALSO BY

For more books by Poppy Bridgeman

scan the QR code below.

ABOUT POPPY BRIDGEMAN

Hi, I'm Poppy Bridgeman, the cozy mystery alter ego of Canadian author P A Wilson. Poppy was "born" because sometimes stories need a gentler touch—with a little magic, a dash of humor, and plenty of sleuthing spirit.

As Poppy, I write the *Witch of Henbane Island* series (where witches and festivals collide with mysteries), the *EB Eats Culinary Mysteries* (a small-town diner, a determined heroine, and murder on the menu), and the *Pages & Paws Bookstore Mysteries* (a Devon bookshop, two mischievous corgis, and plenty of secrets tucked between the shelves).

When I'm not tangled in my characters' escapades, I'm happily tangled in yarn—I knit, weave, and doodle in sketchbooks between writing sessions. I also love to travel, finding inspiration for charming settings, quirky characters, and suspicious strangers wherever I go.

Home base is the Vancouver area, where I juggle writing as both Poppy and P A Wilson. Whichever name is on the cover, I'm always chasing the next story.

ACKNOWLEDGMENTS

Writing may look like a solitary pursuit, but I could never do this alone. I've been lucky to have support, encouragement, and inspiration from so many corners that it's impossible to thank everyone properly—but I'll try.

My writing groups keep me sharp and creative: The Vancouver Writers Social Group challenges me to see stories in new ways, The Royal City Literary Arts Society has given me the chance to learn from generous and talented writers, and The Other 11 Months group reminds me that words on the page are what really matter. My critique partners, with their sharp eyes and honest feedback, make sure each story is the best version it can be.

And of course, my heartfelt thanks to my beta readers. You catch the wobbly bits, cheer for the good ones, and remind me that these stories aren't just mine—they're meant for you, my readers.